The Spy Gate Liars

A New Sherlock Holmes Mystery

Note to Readers:

Your enjoyment of this new Sherlock Holmes mystery will be enhanced by re-reading the original story that inspired this one –

The Reigate Squires

It has been appended and may be found in the back portion of this book.

The Spy Gate Liars

A New Sherlock Holmes Mystery

Craig Stephen Copland

Copyright © 2017 by Craig Stephen Copland

Published by:

Conservative Growth
1101 30th Street NW. Ste. 500
Washington, DC 20007

Cover design by Rita Toews.

ISBN-13: 978-1544089614

ISBN-10: 1544089619

Dedication

To the orphans of war.

Acknowledgments

Like all writers of Sherlock Holmes fan fiction, I owe a debt to Sir Arthur Conan Doyle. Or, if you are a true Sherlockian, to Dr. John Watson, who recorded the brilliant exploits of the world's most famous detective. This particular novella is a tribute to the original story, *The Reigate Squires*.

The events of this story take place in France and England. I have had many wonderful adventures in those countries and am grateful for the wonderful friends and colleagues with whom I shared them.

A special thanks is given to my dear friend, Mary Engelking, who yet again shared ideas and improvements for the story and encourages me to keep on writing Sherlocks.

Several fellow writers read draft versions of this story and made valuable edits and suggestions, mostly related to sections that needed to be cut. My thanks to all of them, particularly those in the Tokyo Writers Workshop, whose insights and suggestions I will miss now that I no longer live in that incredible city

I also acknowledge the dear friends and family who continue to encourage me in this pleasant if quixotic quest of writing a new mystery to correspond to every story in the original Canon.

Contents

Chapter One
Rushing to Nancy

Crossing the Channel on a fine morning in the early spring of '87, with the sun shining over a calm sea, the breeze in my face, and the white cliffs of Dover fading behind me, should have been an uplifting experience to my soul.

But I was worried sick.

I had not slept a wink the night before. At six o'clock that morning, I had rushed out of our rooms on Baker Street, shouted at the cab driver to hurry to Victoria Station, and then stood and paced up and down the railway platform waiting for the first train to Dover.

Now I was pacing fore and aft on the deck of the Dover to Calais ferry, knowing full well that my doing so would not speed the boat up in the least.

The reason for my distress was in my pocket; a telegram that had arrived in the late afternoon of the previous day. It ran:

Cher Docteur Watson:

Votre ami, M. Sherlock Holmes est très malade. Il est à l'article de la morte. Veuillez vous rendre à Nancy dans les plus brefs délais.

Dr. Alphonse Stoskopff

Médicin du garde

Hotel Grand Dulong

Place Stanislas, Nancy

I had immediately sent a return telegram to the house doctor demanding more information but had received no reply, which was not at all surprising as French doctors seldom work past five o'clock, even if they do not get back to their wives before seven.

Holmes never took sick. His constitution was made of iron and I had, in utter amazement, observed him over the past few years as he went without sleep for days on end, kept alive only by tobacco and coffee, when in hot, intense pursuit of a case.

During the past several months he had worked non-stop all over Europe identifying one criminal after another who was part of the notorious *Trapani Mandamento,* and seeing them off to prison or the gallows. As he had begun to pull on one strand of their web of underworld enterprises, he continued to discover yet another dastardly activity. Arms and armaments were being illegally sold across borders for the equipping of any anarchist group who placed an order for them. Young women and even some young men had been smuggled in from India for immoral purposes. Bank vaults had been broken into without the bankers' noticing until the money was long gone. Holmes methodically unwound each of the intricate plots and solved the mysteries.

Far from wearing him down, it invigorated him. He sent brief notes affirming that he was beside himself with zealous satisfaction, hardly able to contain his sheer joy, and grudgingly taking only an hour or two of sleep when sitting in a train cabin. He was utterly and completely alive.

For Sherlock Holmes to be near death was unheard of, and I feared that he had been poisoned by some fiend. I had packed my medical bag full of every known antidote for every deadly concoction that could have been administered to him unawares, and I hoped and prayed that he had not succumbed already.

Long before the ferry alarm sounded announcing our pending arrival at the port of Calais, I was standing in the front of the line at the exit, ready to rush off and run across the center of the town to the railway station. As soon as the stevedores lowered the wide gangplank, I was on my way. Calais is, like the rest of France, supremely unorganized and the docks greeted me with a cacophony of peddlers, swindlers, touts, illicit appeals, and cab drivers who I was sure would take over an hour to deliver me to the train station. I was having none of it. I trusted my shoe leather and walked smartly through the streets, past the great lighthouse, and on to the train station a few blocks to the south. By the time I arrived on the platform, I was breathing heavily and sweating, but I was in time for the 12:45 train to Paris, Gare du Nord. I purchased a ticket and found my seat with just a few minutes to spare and permitted myself a brief interval of reflection. In my mind, I reviewed all the most common poisons I knew of and their treatment. My medical case was opened and closed thrice as I checked yet again to make sure that I had packed the appropriate medications.

Twelve forty-five came and went. So also did one o'clock and the train did not move. I had not traveled much on the Continent but Holmes had advised me on numerous occasions that trains in England at least make an effort to be on time. Those in Germany always arrive and depart on the exact minute. French trains, however, leave at random when the conductor has finished his lunch. The French were, to their credit, more reliable than the Spanish or Italians whose trains might or might not adhere to the day let alone to the hour on the schedule.

The train did eventually depart from the station and rolled along over the hills and fields of Picardie. I chatted on and off with my seatmate, who seemed just a bit too inquisitive for my taste. Holmes had warned me that all Frenchmen were either spies or wished they were, and I was undecided whether or not this chap was being friendly or an agent of Holmes's enemies.

I was relieved when we finally pulled into the Gare du Nord. Baedecker had recommended a small *pension* conveniently located halfway between the Gare du Nord and the Gare de l'Est, where I would depart from the next morning. I gave my name to the desk, not thinking for a moment that doing so might not be the best idea. The fellow behind the desk immediately looked up at me and broke into a broad grin.

"*Mon dieu. Vraiment*, le Docteur Watson? The writer? The writer of the stories of the Sherlock Holmes? *Merveilleux.*"

He turned and retreated into his inner office and came back

bearing a copy of *Les Aventures de M. Sherlock Holmes*. I was not aware that my publisher had arranged for a French translation of my stories and for a brief, fleeting moment thought that I might soon see another strand of royalties coming from the Continent when it occurred to me that what I was looking at was no doubt a pirated copy. I was fit to be tied and was tempted to rip the chap's book into pieces, but he was not the culprit and had likely purchased the book in good faith. So I signed his copy and smiled back at him.

The following morning, I departed early and walked the block to the great Gare de l'Est and boarded my train to Nancy. I tried to force myself to relax but my mind was racing and I could not stop worrying about Holmes. I found myself condemning my ignoring his earlier letters and telegrams. Surely I should have seen in them hints that he could be in danger. He had no close friends in the world other than me and I felt a deep responsibility to care for his physical well-being. I feared that I had let him down.

These unpleasant thoughts were only banished from my mind when I descended from the train in Nancy, an ancient town in the far east of France. Before the war between France and Prussia, it was still some fifty miles from the border with the German states but with the German annexing of Alsace, Nancy was now the closest French town to the frontier. I knew little about it other than what I had read in Baedeker.

The Grand Hotel Dulong occupied the far corner of the central square and, with its ornate façade and rows of large windows, appeared to be the best accommodation in the town. If Holmes was going to die, he at least had picked an elegant hotel in which to do so.

"Good morning," I said to the man behind the hotel desk. My French is weak and I am of the firm belief, proven during my years under the Raj, that anyone in the world can understand plain English as long as it is spoken loudly and enunciated clearly. "I am here to see one of your guests, a Monsieur Sherlock Holmes."

The fellow was visibly startled and without saying a word, turned and retreated to the hotel offices. Two minutes later he reappeared, followed by a nattily dressed man of about the same age as me.

"Ah, Docteur Watson. Vous êtes arrivés. Dieu merci. Venez avec moi tout de suite."

I assumed that this must be the house doctor and I followed him up the staircase to the third floor. He used a pass key and ushered me into a spacious a room that would have been filled with sunlight passing through the large windows had they not been entirely covered with dark curtains. On the far wall was a double bed and under some blankets was a hump that I concluded must be the semi-comatose body of Sherlock Holmes. The doctor opened one set of drapes and allowed the light to enter. Then he went to the bedside and gently rocked Holmes's right shoulder.

"M'sieur Holmes. M'sieur Holmes. Réveillez-vous. Votre ami, Docteur Watson, est ici pour vous. Réveillez-vous."

Holmes moved very slowly and struggled to raise his upper body to a sitting position.

Good heavens, I thought to myself. He looked utterly ghastly. His face was inflamed and there were horrible dark circles under his sunken eyes. His lips were gray. He was blinking his eyes as if he could not clear his vision. As he raised his hand and pointed his finger at me, I could see him grimacing in pain. Mentally, I was making note of his symptoms and trying to assign them to the effects of one poison or other, but he seemed to have been afflicted by more than one horrible potion and I could not decide which of them to try to treat first.

"Waaaatson," his feeble voice said. "Is…that…you?"

"Yes, Holmes. It is me."

"Ohhh…how good of you…to come. You may tell…the hotel doctor…to go…and do thank him." After uttering the final word, I heard a terrible long wheeze and assumed that his respiratory system had also been attacked.

I turned to Doctor Alphonse.

"Merci, very much, my ami. You may departez now. I will look after Monsieur Holmes."

The doctor took a few steps back from the bed but did not turn to leave the room. Holmes raised his trembling hand and waved feebly to him.

"Thank you…doctor…you have been very kind…please let my own doctor attend to me." This utterance was followed by another extended wheeze.

"Waaaatson… in the loo…there are towels…please soak one in cold water…and bring it to me…I am burning up."

I went immediately into the adjoining lavatory and ran cold water over a small towel and brought it back to Holmes. The hotel doctor was still in the room.

I placed the wet towel in Holmes's shaking hand and turned to the hotel doctor, thanking him again. In a friendly manner, I took his elbow and directed him to the door. He was obviously reluctant to leave the room and so I was forced to deliver instructions in English.

"Mr. Holmes wishes to be left alone with me. We thank you for your kind attention. I will look after the bill for your services when I pay for my room. Thank you, sir."

I walked beside him until he had departed and the door was closed. On turning to Holmes I saw him dabbing his face with the towel.

"Haaaas he…gone?" The voice was muffled by the towel that was now covering his face.

"Yes. It is just you and me in the room now."

"Pleeeeease…lock the door."

This seemed a strange request as we did not appear to be in any danger, but I did as he had asked.

"The door has been secured, Holmes. Now put the towel down and let me have a look at you."

The towel was immediately placed on the bed and I was horrified by the discolored blotches that had stained it. On looking up from it, I stared into the beaming, healthy, smiling face of Sherlock Holmes. He immediately swung his legs over the side of the bed and stepped toward me. Both his hands clasped my shoulders.

"Watson, Watson. My dear, dear chap. I am so sorry to have given you such distress and brought you all the way across France. I had no idea that a French doctor would think to call in an English one. But it was so good of you to come, my friend."

"Good heavens, Holmes!" I exploded. "What in the world are you trying to do? You had me convinced that you were at death's door. What is the meaning of this nonsense?"

He smiled warmly and tenderly at me and I knew I could not remain angry with him for long.

"Ah, my friend," he said. "These borderlands between France and Germany are a hotbed of spies and counterspies. The French have spies everywhere and so do the Germans. Like the Cretans, all Alsatians are liars and are either spies or are pretending they are. They have been on me like a plague of fleas for several weeks. The only way I have been able to gather any data or do any investigating is to feign sickness all day long and slip out through the service entrance after five o'clock. But do sit down and have a brandy and let me explain."

I was still shaking my head in amazement. Holmes had tricked me more than once in the past with his disguises, but never had I been so thoroughly taken in as I had been on walking into a hotel room in the eastern frontier of France.

"The French," he began, "do make an excellent brandy. Allow me to pour one for each of us. You deserve one for all your troubles on my behalf."

We took our seats in two comfortable chairs. I loosened my collar and tie and Holmes, still in his housecoat, lit his pipe.

"I have been doing a bit of work for the French *Ministre des Affaires étrangères*. It was not covered by the press in London, so you are not likely aware that so far this year five former German army officers have been murdered."

That was serious, but it made no sense to me.

"You said," I said, "that you were hired by the *French*. Why would they care if the Germans lost an officer or two? I would have thought they would be rather pleased. There does not appear to be any love lost between the two countries after their war."

"Excellent observation," said Holmes. "But the chaps in Berlin, right up to Otto what's-his-name, are placing the blame on the French. You know how they are about honor and seeking revenge and all that. The Germans are threatening, quietly so far, that they might go to war again if the Frenchies do not stop killing off their men. The chaps at the Quay d'Orsay really do not want another war, regardless of their posing in the name of French honor. They lost the last one rather badly, a *folie de grandeur* I believe it what they called it. They had to give up the entire province of Alsace and were generally humiliated.

"Those French chaps are insisting that they are not behind it, but who else could it be? So they have hired me to find out who is doing it and make them stop. It has all been quite fascinating, but I am not even close to solving the crime, and every time I turn around I find some spy—French, German, Alsatian—on my tail. I detest having my every move recorded and reported on and so the ruse of feigning ill. I am terribly sorry, my friend, for having disrupted your medical practice but I must say that I am thrilled to have you here. Your assistance will be invaluable."

"And what," I asked, "do you expect me to do? I came prepared to attend to your physical ailments, not to go gallivanting around the far regions of France after dark."

Holmes smiled and was on the verge of laughing at me.

"Of course you did, but you and I know full well that you become bored quickly with your patients and cannot resist the adventure. And I am quite certain that at the bottom of your medical bag lies your service revolver that you packed just in case. Am I right?"

Of course, he was right. He invariably was. And I must admit that I involuntarily smiled back at him.

Chapter Two
The Cat Burglar

"When do we start?" I asked.

"It would be very helpful if you could begin straight away. Your presence here is a godsend and allows me to banish the overly attentive house doctor from this room, demanding that I only be seen by you. Might I suggest that you go now into the village market and procure several days supply of fresh fruit and vegetables and then announce to the hotel desk that you have diagnosed me with some horribly deadly and contagious disease that might be overcome by healthy eating, but other than seeing you I must be quarantined for the sake of the health of the village children. You can make up something like that, I am sure."

"There is no known contagious disease that is cured by fresh fruit and vegetables," I objected.

"Then make one up. How about ... oh ... *Llasa Double Pulmonary Fever?* That should do it. Terribly contagious. The virulent Tibetan strain, not the African one. I contracted it years ago whilst in Tibet and it recurs every so often, much like malaria only potentially fatal."

"But how then," I asked, "am I to be spared contracting it from you?"

"Good heavens, Watson. Use your imagination. Say that you were also stricken with it whilst you were in Tibet but recovered fully and are now immune."

"But I have never been in Tibet," I said.

"My dear chap, we are making this up. It is quite acceptable to imagine Tibet if you are going to imagine the disease itself out of whole cloth."

"Oh ... yes. I see your point. I suppose I could do that. And then what happens?"

"We will wait until after five o'clock. At that time all of the spies, as required by their unions, leave their posts, visit their mistresses, and then go home to their wives and children. We will be able to exit through the back of the hotel, find our dinner in one of the many pleasant cafés, and then attempt to break into one of the finer homes in this town. Now please, on your way. The market is a block to the south of the square. And kindly refrain from the appalling French practice of holding baguettes in your armpit."

I did as requested and returned to the hotel with several sacks of perfectly formed fresh fruits and vegetables. At the hotel desk, I explained the circumstances of Holmes's quarantine to the staff, for good measure adding that one of the consequences of the horrid disease was what the French referred to as *couper le pin,* a non-medical term that I was sure our inquisitive house doctor would take note of, assuming that he did not wish to be impotent for the remainder of his days.

Over a brief repast of *foie gras,* brandy, and baguettes, Holmes provided a few more details of our mission.

"Five men, all former officers in the Prussian army, have been killed. The most recent were two men who had been living here in Nancy. Two weeks ago, the chaps at the Quay d'Orsay requested my assistance. My sleuthing to date has confirmed that all five of them served in the war and were part of the same battalion. Since arriving here in Nancy, I have discovered the location of the houses in which the murders took place. Each house was the abode of the deceased, and this evening you are I are going to pay a visit to them. We are too late to do an examination of the body and the site of the crime, but we need to learn how it was that the killer entered the house, committed the crime, and then escaped."

"Are you saying," I asked, "that they were murdered in their own homes?"

"Precisely. Not in a tavern or a brothel as is customary when the French are disposing of unwelcome Germans, but in their homes, in their bedrooms, and late at night after the household staff had gone to bed. There were no reports of a struggle, no cries of pain, no doors slammed."

"That is most peculiar," I said.

"And that is why it makes for a most fascinating case. But come now, we must don our disguises so that we will not be recognized as Englishmen as we wander the dark streets of Nancy."

From his valise, he procured a black tam, a cravat, and a thin theatrical mustache.

I put them on and regarded myself in the mirror.

"Would you not agree," said Holmes, "that you now look like a highly typical mid-level functionary of the French municipal administration?"

"I would say I looked more like a comic buffoon *poseur* seen on stage in the West End," I replied.

"Correct, and a redundancy," said Holmes.

It was dark by the time we had departed from the hotel and found a delightful dinner in a local café. Holmes led me along several tree-lined streets until we were in an obviously better-off neighborhood. He stopped at a perimeter fence of a large three-story house. The fence was made of steel stakes, all painted black, and topped with gold-colored sharp spear tips.

"Somehow," said Holmes, "the killer must have been able to scale this fence, enter the house late at night, find his way to the third floor, and murder the victim as he lay in his bed."

"How did he kill him? You said that no shots were heard."

"Every one of them was stabbed in the eye with a dagger."

"That is again most peculiar," I said.

"Precisely. What is inexplicable is that in all reports from the coroner it notes that there was also a small wound above the eye and the larger penetration directly into the eye socket."

"Hmm, very peculiar," I said, repeating myself. "I suppose it is possible that the first attempt might have failed and the second succeeded."

"Come, come, my dear Watson. Once perhaps. But four times? Impossible."

Holmes now turned and grasped a fence stake in each hand,

glanced up and down the structure and then turned to me.

"Let us see if we can repeat his moves. This may require some gymnastics on our part, but if you will drop to one knee and allow me to step from your leg to your shoulder and then stand up, I should be able to straddle this fearsome fence without impaling myself."

I did as requested and soon was on my feet with Holmes standing on my shoulder with one foot and swinging his leg, unimpeded, over the top of the fence.

"Now," he said, "press your body up against the fence and I will be able to use your shoulders again as a ladder on my way back down."

I pushed myself flat against the stakes and felt the toe of his boot slip through the gap and settle on my shoulder. The other foot followed, and then he gave a jump and landed on the ground on the other side.

"That was," I said, "all well and good, but what am I now supposed to do? I do not believe that we can do the same maneuver with you on that side and me on this."

"An excellent observation, Watson. So I suggest that you walk around to the main gate and I will unlock it and let you in. There is no sentry on duty after seven o'clock."

A few minutes later both of us were standing against the back wall of the large house trying to discern how a killer could possibly have broken in without making a disturbance. The windows on the ground floor were all locked and protected by rows of metal bars. The back door was secured by a lock that Holmes himself admitted would be difficult to pick. The only access to the second floor would have required an individual who was more ape than man and able to climb drainpipes and cling to protruding bricks with only his fingertips.

"The killer," concluded Holmes, "appears to have the skills of a cat burglar. He had to both ascend the wall and then open the window whilst hanging on with one hand. Quite the exceptional adversary we are up against."

For the next fifteen minutes. Holmes paced back and forth around the house, sometimes stopping and closing his eyes in deep concentration, then shaking his head and pacing some more. With a final shake of his head, he turned to me.

"I am as of yet still in a fog," he said. "But come, we shall pay a visit to the second house."

Through several blocks of the dark residential streets of Nancy, we wandered until Holmes stopped in front of another elegant home.

This second house, the one in which another former Prussian army officer had been murdered a week earlier, was likewise a formidable obstacle for any nocturnal invasion. Instead of a fence, it was surrounded by a thick and impenetrable wall of Russian Olive trees, all planted tightly together and with horrible thorns ready to stop even the most determined of thieves or killers. There was no sign anywhere on the perimeter of the branches having been cut away to permit passage.

"The only way he could have entered," mused Holmes, "was by way of the front gate. But the structure is high and formidable. This chap must be quite the monkey to have managed such a feat."

Again, Holmes walked slowly around the house, stopping constantly to do a close examination of the impenetrable thorny hedge. Each time, he shook his head and muttered, "Impossible."

By midnight we were heading back to the hotel. Holmes walked in silence, his head cast down, his hands in his pockets, and his chin almost touching his sternum.

"Data," he said. "I am starving for data. Whenever a murder is committed, there are clues to be unearthed all over the place. So far, I have not had access to the scenes of the crimes until far too late after the fact. There are so many questions to which I need answers before I can even start to form a hypothesis."

"Very well then," I said. "Since you have conscripted me for this undertaking, would you mind terribly telling me what data you do have. So far I am blind as a mole except for observing an ingenious method of scaling a dangerous fence."

"Oh," he said. "I must say that you have a point there, Watson. Let me tell you what I know so far from my initial investigations. I do not expect any imaginative insights from you, but your simple questions have at times been useful in directing my thoughts in a new way. So, yes. Here is what we know so far.

"All five of the victims were of about the same age, rather close to forty. All had served in Bismarck's army during the last war, the one we refer to as the Franco-Prussian conflict. I have discovered that all of them were part of the same *Kompanie* in the Prussian army when it invaded Alsace. Thus, it stands to reason that the motive for their murders is tied to something that took place during that war. But there could be a hundred possibilities. Dark secrets hidden; money or jewels squirrelled away; embarrassing secrets of intrigue; revenge … the list is long."

"Were those chaps the only young officers of their unit?" I asked.

"No, they were part of a unit that included at least three others. One, I have traced up the road to Strasbourg, a Charles Friedel, and another one now lives in England. The third cannot yet be found. I suspect that the fellow in Strasbourg is now in fear for his life and we must pay him a visit before the nimble assassin gets to him."

"When?"

Holmes appeared to ponder my question for a moment.

"If we leave in the morning, our departure will be noted by the legion of spies that infest this town, so we best depart again in the late afternoon. Strasbourg is only a few hours by train and we should be there in sufficient time to alert the chap and advise him to vacate his house if he has been so unwise not to have already done so."

I slept soundly that night, weary from the lack of sleep the previous night and my worried travels. Once during the middle of the night, I heard footsteps going back and forth along the hallway outside my room and concluded that Holmes was pacing whilst trying to put together the pieces of the puzzle.

The following day we spent in our adjoining rooms. I used the time to review and improve my latest story about the adventures of my friend and now famous detective. Twice during the day, I checked in on my friend to make sure that he was at least eating something nourishing. On both occasions I found him in one of the armchairs, his legs folded and drawn up under him, his hands together with his fingertips touching, and his eyes closed. I knew not to disturb him with conversation but was satisfied that the bowl of fruit and platter of cold cuts appeared to have been partially diminished.

At one minute after five o'clock, he tapped quietly on my door.

"Come, Watson. The game is afoot. Off to Strasbourg. Please, quickly don your disguise and we shall be out of Nancy long before we are missed."

I did as requested and we strolled in the fashion of unhurried French bureaucrats to the railway station and boarded the train to Strasbourg. Once on the train, we removed our disguises and became English tourists. The German border agents were suspicious of

French travelers but usually welcoming to the English, what with their Kaiser being the grandson of our beloved Queen and all.

By the time we reached our destination, the sun had set. From the *Bahnhof Straßburg*, we walked a few blocks past the great Cathedral to a hotel that struck me as having been imported from Tudor England. It was quite a popular place nonetheless and Holmes and I were required to share a double room.

"Our lodgings," said Holmes, who appeared to be familiar with the establishment, "are old but very comfortable. I suspect that this city has as many spies as did Nancy but no one has followed us and we will be undetected here until we pay a visit to our monsieur first thing in the morning."

He was wrong.

At seven o'clock in the morning, we were awakened by a loud knocking on our door. I quickly leapt from the bed, pulled a dressing gown over my pajamas and started toward the door.

"Psst!" came an alert from Holmes. "Your revolver," he whispered.

I hastened back to my doctor's bag and slipped the gun into my pocket before opening the door.

"*Guten Morgan, Herr Doktor,*" said the chap in the hall. "*Bitte,* please come with *herr* Sherlock Holmes. Come quickly, please to room *dreihundert vierzehn*. We have need of your services. *Bitte, sofort.*"

I turned and looked at Holmes, who shrugged and gave me instruction.

"Tell him that we will be there as soon as we dress."

"I thought you said that we were not followed," I said.

"It is possible that I underestimated the diligence of the German spies. But let us go and see what their problem is."

Chapter Three
Death in Strasbourg

Room 314 was in another wing of the hotel. Standing at the door were two rather impressive looking German chaps with *Polizei* emblazoned on their uniforms. I greeted them but, as should be expected from the Germans, they merely glared at me and said nothing. One of them opened the door and gestured to us to enter.

Several men were standing in the room and I quickly understood the reason for our having been summoned. Lying in the bed was a body and the area around the pillow was covered with blood. One did not have to be Sherlock Holmes to put together what must have taken place during the night.

A tall blond and broad-shouldered police officer approached Holmes.

"Herr Sherlock Holmes," he said. "I am Hauptkommissar Max Ballauf of the Police of Strasburg. Not coincidental is it that you are staying at this hotel? The case that of you is being investigated has to you been delivered. In the bed is Herr Charles Friedal, and dead he is. Stabbed in the eye, like all of the others. We are made aware of your reputation and welcome your assistance in the solving of this crime."

Without another word he stood back and pointed Holmes toward the bed and the body. I followed.

The unfortunate victim was a man in his mid to late forties and in rather good physical condition. If one can judge by his hair style and facial hair, one might assume that he was a former military officer. His eye socket was gory and now blackening with the dried blood. Curiously, he also had a wound to his eyebrow. There was no doubt as to how he had died. A dagger must have been inserted into his eye and pushed through to his brain. Death would have been almost immediate.

Holmes had taken out his glass and took a full half hour to examine the body, the bed, and the room. I noticed him paying close attention to several deposits of tobacco ash and some sort of German word scratched into the top of the bedside table.

"Commissar Ballauf," he said. "Did one of your men or the hotel staff open the window?"

"Nein. It was open we arrived. The maids reported hearing some disturbance being made in this room just after one o'clock in the morning, felt herself concerned, and came to knock on the door to make sure the guest was not having difficulties. There was no answer and they departed. Herr Friedal had ordered early morning coffee and strudel to be delivered at five thirty. He did not make an answer at the door when the maid arrived and she used her key to make it open. As soon as she saw what had happened she rushes out and runs to the nearest police station. I am called and, knowing that you were staying in the same hotel, I give instructions that nothing in the room be disturbed. Everything is as you see it. The window was open."

Holmes walked over to the window and leaned out. The morning sun had risen and I could see that the window opened to the courtyard below. Once Holmes had withdrawn, I also peered out and observed an entirely unobstructed wall of the building, four stories above the ground level. The only uneven features of the wall were the dark planks that had been affixed to the stucco, giving the hotel its distinctive Tudor appearance. If our killer had entered by the window, he must have been exceptionally adept at scaling walls. A *cat* indeed.

"The staff of the hotel," said the Commissar, "claim that no one suspicious comes into the hotel after eleven o'clock. He must have climbed up the wall and made the window open. No other explanation am I seeing."

I looked at Holmes and detected the familiar unmistakable faint trace of a smile on his face. "*Aha,*" I said to myself. He's on to something.

"I am honored," he said to the police officer, "to have been invited to assist in this case. I will continue my investigation and report to you tomorrow morning if that is acceptable to you. Your station, I believe, is located just east of the cathedral, is it not?"

"Ja. There it is."

"Splendid. I shall report in at eight o'clock tomorrow morning."

Holmes then turned to me, smiled and nodded and walked toward the door.

Once we were out of earshot, I demanded an explanation for the smile that had broadened into a grin.

"I was thinking how a fine cup of German coffee and a generous slice of *brötchen* would make for a delectable breakfast. Perhaps a hard-boiled egg or two. What say, Watson?"

"Enough, Holmes," I replied. "I did not come racing to the Continent to be teased."

"Oh, very well. Let us find a pleasant café and I will be more forthcoming once breakfast is served."

After crossing over the Rhine, we found a pleasant café not far from the palace. We English consider German coffee to be a close cousin to sealant for Macadam, but in small sips it is quite palatable. We sat in silence until we had finished our breakfast and then Holmes again smiled at me in the condescending manner to which I have become accustomed even if annoyed.

"You inspected the pierced eye socket, did you not?" he said.

"I did. Obviously stabbed with a dagger through to the brain."

"And was the eye open or closed when stabbed?"

I had to stop and think about that one. "Open," I said, "there was no damage to the eyelid. But that is very odd. What man just lies on his back and looks at a dagger as his assailant is about to plunge it into his eye?"

"Very odd, indeed," said Holmes. "And the wound above the eye? What of that?"

I had taken a close look at it as well and was only a bit less perplexed.

"It did not appear to be from the dagger as it was not a single cut. Rather it was more like a triangle, as if a small chisel had been pushed into the skin."

"Excellent. And that is the first calling card left behind," said Holmes.

"What are you talking about?" I demanded.

"Come now, Watson. Where have you observed a triangle and an eye in close proximity to each other?

I thought for a moment and then it came to me.

"On the back of the American dollar bill?"

"Precisely. And to which fraternal organization does that symbol belong?"

"The Masons," I said.

"And they wish to let us and all other inquirers know that they are behind these killings."

"Why would they do that?" I asked.

"That, we do not yet know. But let us move on to the other evidence. How might the killer have gained entry?" he asked.

"If no one was observed coming or going past the front desk, then he must have come through the window."

"Precisely. That is exactly what the killer wishes us to believe. And even you could tell that unless we are dealing with someone with superhuman skills in scaling walls, that is impossible."

"How then?"

"Through the door."

I shook my head in disbelief. Holmes smiled at me yet again.

"I believe that I have said to you before, that once you eliminate all other ..."

"Confound you, Holmes!" I said. "I know what you have said countless times. But the staff reported no one coming or going late in the evening. So that is impossible."

"No, my dear chap. The staff reported that they saw no *suspicious men* entering or leaving late in the evening or in the early hours of the morning. However, we know that in every hotel in the civilized world there are certain people who *do* enter and leave during those hours but are not considered suspicious. And who might those people be, my good man?"

The answer was obvious. "Prostitutes," I said. "Are you saying that a *woman* was the murderer?"

"There was," he said, "a faint scent of perfume on the pillow. Not something a German man would ever dream of putting on himself."

"So you believe that a woman entered the room and then stabbed these chaps? They were all former soldiers. They could have easily defended themselves against a woman."

"Of course they could, if only they were thinking and behaving rationally during the seconds before one eyeball was so violently abused. And, furthermore, did you notice what the chap was wearing."

I had noticed and said that he must have been very tired to fall into bed without changing into his bedclothes.

"Tired enough not to have removed his shoes?" Holmes queried.

He did not permit me to answer but carried on.

"He had removed his suit jacket and his cravat. His shirt and his trousers were somewhat disheveled. He was obviously in a physical state that led him to momentarily close his eyes, permitting his killer to stab him with no defense having been thought necessary."

"What sort of horrible, evil woman would do such a thing?" I said.

Holmes smiled, leaned back in his chair and folded his arms across his chest.

"I have heard some rumors," he said. "Prior to this morning I considered them without credence, but my thoughts are changing. There have been stories circulating throughout the police services and press of Europe of a young woman who works in secret as a paid assassin. She is reported to be stunningly beautiful, a master of the art of seduction, irresistible to susceptible males, and utterly ruthless. These murders may be her handiwork."

"Who is she?" I asked.

"She is known as Annie Morrison and is said to come from America, but no one knows for sure. Some stories have her as French, others as German, others yet as Italian. She could easily have passed as a woman of the evening and entered and left any fine hotel along with a score of other such ladies without causing any suspicion."

"Who paid her?"

"The Masons, most likely. Or perhaps some renegade lodge of their organization. Generally, they do not engage in murder. Extortion is their preferred method of accumulating wealth, which is why so many of them own banks."

"Well then," I said, "if you know who she is and she does not yet know about you, it should not be all that difficult to track her down."

"On the contrary, my good man," replied Holmes. "She knows that I am on her trail."

"How can you say that?"

"Her calling cards."

"What are you talking about?"

"The tobacco ash."

"Holmes, enough."

"On the coffee table in the hotel room, there were four distinct little piles of tobacco ash."

"Which means," I said, "that she smokes and, being American, is not well-mannered enough to use the ash tray but drops the drops the ashes on the table."

Holmes chuckled. "Would it were only that. But each of the four deposits was a different ash. One was Virginia Gold, one from a French *Gitaines,* one was a Burley blend from Turkey, and the fourth a rather vile, rough monstrosity favored by the Australians."

Yet again, my observation was, "How very peculiar."

"And the word scratched into the lacquer on the table. Did you read what it said?"

I acknowledged that I had glanced at it but could not decipher what is said.

"It was hastily scratched," said Holmes, "but it appears that it was the word *rache.*"

I was startled. "Why that's the same word that Jefferson Hope wrote on the wall years ago. What a bizarre coincidence. So this is all about revenge as well."

He gave me yet another of his condescending smiles.

"Not at all, my friend. This brazen fiend is taunting me. Like every criminal in England or America, she has read your romanticized sensational story about our *Study in Scarlet* and she is obviously aware of my monograph on the one hundred and forty varieties of tobacco ash. So she is rubbing my nose in it. She is utterly daring me to try to track her down and stop her."

"Can you?"

"In my entire career, I have only been bested by one woman, *the woman,* and it shall not happen again. Irene Adler was a noble woman in her own right. This woman is a cold-blooded assassin, and I will see her hang for her deeds."

The smile had long departed Holmes's face and in its place was a set jaw, eyes as hard as steel, and a furrowed brow. As he spoke his fists slowly clenched until his knuckles whitened. The assassin who had hunted down these soldiers had become the hunted.

The pleasant interlude that we had enjoyed over coffee on at the edge of the Rhine had vanished. Without saying anything, Holmes rose from the table, left some coins beside the unfinished breakfast and turned and walked away. I hastened to follow him.

"What now?" I asked.

"Back to England."

"Pardon me if I ask why. She's killing Germans in France and Alsace. Why England?"

"Because that is where she will strike next."

"Enough, Holmes. Explain."

He immediately stopped his hurried pace and turned to me, forcing a smile.

"Forgive me, my dear chap. My manners hare been terrible. I will explain. Among the young officers who were part of the battalion that occupied Metz, there were the five who are already murdered. The only other one I have identified is a fellow named Maurice Kellerman. He moved to England immediately after leaving the Prussian army and changed his name to Morris Cunningham. He is living near Reigate in Surrey and I fully expect that he is next on the list to be assassinated. Our assassin is likely already on her way there. We need to get there as soon as possible. Our taking our time to come to Strasbourg has meant that we were not able to stop the murder of Friedal. I do not plan to make that same mistake again."

He turned and resumed his forced march back to the hotel.

"But," I protested, "you told the Commissar that you would report to him tomorrow morning."

Holmes slowed his pace. "Yes … I suppose I did. Would you mind terribly sending him a note explaining that we were called away suddenly and that we will wire a full report from London."

"What reason can I give?"

"Good heavens, Watson. Use your imagination. Make something up. And while you are at it, please send a telegram to Mr. Cunningham in Reigate warning him to take precautions for his life and advising him that we are on our way as quickly as possible."

He resumed his near run until we reached the hotel.

Chapter Four
Return to Surrey to Stop a Murder

We departed from the hotel in full view of the desk and any spies that might have been watching us and rushed to the train station. Travel from Alsace, across France, and then back to England took two full days. This time it was Holmes who paced back and forth on the deck of the ferry whilst I scribbled away in the cabin. Upon arrival in Dover we spent the night in a local hotel and first thing the next morning we boarded a train to Surrey. By early afternoon we had arrived at the station in Reigate.

"Mr. Sherlock Holmes and Dr. Watson," spoke a voice from behind us as we entered the station. We turned to face a tall, gaunt man who was formally dressed. His face, elongated and jaundiced, was a mask of impassivity.

"Yes," replied Holmes, "and who might you be?"

"My name, sir, is William Kirwan. I am in service to the Squires Cunningham. I have been sent by him to bring you to the manor. Kindly follow me please, gentleman."

He said nothing more but reached for our valises and, taking one in each hand, turned and walked toward to roadway in front of the station. There was an elegant closed carriage standing there, attended to by a uniformed driver and a gleaming brace of black horses. Mr. Kirwan passed the luggage to the driver and then opened the carriage door.

We stepped up and inside and he followed, placing himself on the comfortable bench seat opposite Holmes and me. I heard the driver give a shout to the horses and we were underway.

"The drive," said Kirwan, "to the manor will take some twenty minutes. Since time is limited, you will forgive me if I make the most of it. I know who you are, Mr. Holmes, having read all about you in *The Strand,* and in the accounts in the press of your exceptional accomplishments."

Holmes offered a perfunctory smile and began a reply.

"Thank you …"

"It would be," interrupted Kirwan, "a more efficient use of our time if you would not speak but listen and respond to my questions. Thank you."

Holmes stopped speaking and this time gave a nod and a genuine smile.

"I am listening."

"I assume, sir, that you are aware that over the past few years, because of the decline in the value of the pound sterling against several of the European currencies, a distressing number of fine

English estates have been purchased by opportunistic foreigners."

"I am aware of that trend," replied Holmes. "It has been particularly widespread in Surrey. I was not aware, however, of its having become a bone of contention amongst the local populace. The tone of your voice leads me to suspect that it has."

"We're all fair-minded English men and women," said Kirwan. "We respect the French and the Germans and the Dutch and the rest of them, but we are perhaps a little more fond of them when they stay on their side of the Channel than on ours. And we are not at all fond of them when they come over here and take advantage of our good English families, who may have fallen on hard times."

"Are you attempting, Mr. Kirwan," said Holmes, "to allude to some aspects of your employer's undertaking. If you are, then I suggest that you come right out and say so. As you have noted, time is limited. So if you are trying to say something, sir, then say it or quit wasting my time."

The fellow appeared to be a bit taken aback by the bluntness of Holmes's statement and for a few seconds did not respond. Then he gave a nod and continued.

"You have come here because Squire Cunningham *pere* and Squire Cunningham *fils* have engaged your services. Is that correct?"

"No, that is not correct. One: I was not aware that there were two squires, a father and a son. And two: they have not yet requested my services nor have I agreed to have them as my clients."

"That is good news, Mr. Holmes. It is my understanding that you are an honorable man and I can assure you that there are no more dishonorable men in all of Surrey that Messrs. Cunningham and Cunningham."

"That, sir," replied Holmes, "is a surprising comment coming from a man who has been in their service for a long time. The fact that you are you still here leaves me highly skeptical of your probity and your motives."

"As you should be, sir. I assure you that both are above reproach and my comments are for your sake, sir, and not mine. I entered service in the manor twenty years ago. It was owned at that time by Sir Oswald Acton and a more decent man has never walked the face of this earth. It was an honor beyond words for me to be of service to him. Five years ago he entered into a promising business venture that ended up in failure and he suffered enormous financial losses. The strain on him was so great that his heart failed. He passed away and his saintly wife was forced to sell the manor for a pittance but she needed the funds immediately to pay off debts and she took the first offer made to her. It came from a German named Kellerman. At the last minute, he demanded that, as part of the agreement, I and the rest of the staff sign contracts to serve for a minimum of five more years. We were all so devoted to Mrs. Acton, and so desirous to see her relieved of her misery, that we did not hesitate to agree to his terms. Our doing so was a terrible mistake. Should you wish me to disclose matters that are normally kept in confidence, I would agree to do so. I understand from reading Dr. Watson's stories that you are a master at getting staff to reveal confidences about their employers."

"Am I indeed?" said Holmes. "That may be true and I recall numerous times when I had to coax and persuade the household help to take me into their confidence. I do not recall a time when it was volunteered so readily. So please proceed, and do try to be as exact as possible."

The fellow began to speak in measured tones but with each sentence his face became progressively redder and his speech more animated.

"Quite so, sir. Both father and son are vile monsters, utterly lacking in shame, civility, or any normal degree of decency. They are, as I assume you are aware, not even Englishmen. They are immigrants from somewhere on the Continent—Germans, likely—we are not sure. They are most certainly not squires. They falsely appropriated that honorable title in order to give themselves airs. We, the staff of the manor, to a man and a maid, have put an end to that pretense. We have bruited it about the town that they are frauds and to be treated as such."

"I suspect," said Holmes, "that they were not particularly grateful to you for doing so."

"It was done in secret, sir. Were they to know the source, they would seek harsh retribution and they are capable of exacting the same."

"Are they? How might that be so?"

"If anyone in the town dares to cross either of them, they take that person to court on completely false accusations. They use their wealth to hire some unscrupulous lawyers from London and invariably either win their cases or grind their opponents down with ruinous legal costs. They are merciless. The neighboring estate was recently sold to a chap from Leeds, another outsider with money to spare, and no sooner had the ink dried on the deeds than the Cunninghams had launched a suit claiming that they owned a prize section of pasture. They will do anything, *anything*, to have their way and line their pockets."

"They would not be the first wealthy landowners to do so. I can think of several, all Englishmen to the core, who act in the same manner, even to their own English neighbors."

"That is only the beginning of it, Mr. Holmes. Both of them are immoral, lecherous womanizers. The son has already charmed and seduced several of the young maidens in the town, promised them that they would become the lady of the manor, then tossed them aside, ruined for life. The father has acted in a similar manner with three of the widows, each of whom had been left in a financially secure position by a loving husband. But that evil man convinced them that he would be their Lord Protector, had them sign over to him authority for their affairs, drained their accounts, and tossed them aside, utterly heart-broken and impoverished."

"Are the inhabitants of Reigate complete imbeciles?" asked Holmes. "How is it that they have let this go on time after time?"

"The monsters have been brought to a complete halt, sir. But it took time. Young women and widows are alike in the susceptibility to the false charms of a wealthy man. But now their evil deeds are known throughout and no one in the entire town will give them the time of day. Those of us on the staff are counting the days until our years under contract have expired and we can seek positions that afford us some degree of pride and dignity."

The man's fists had clenched as he spoke and he was near apoplectic with anger as he struggled to get the words out. Holmes remained as cool as steel.

"Very well, sir. I take your information under advisement and will govern myself accordingly. I have come to Reigate, however, because it appears that the lives of the squires might be in danger."

"That, sir," Kirwan exploded, "would be most welcomed by all and sundry. I can think of nothing more honorable for a person to do that to cut their throats. Were it not that I have a wife and children to think of, I would gladly do it myself."

With this utterance, the man suddenly seemed to realize that he might have said more than he intended to. He took a deep breath, folded his arms across his chest, and said no more. We continued in silence until we reached our destination.

The entry gate was large and stately, although not particularly fancy. The arch above the drive bore the name *Hills of Lorraine* and the grounds surrounding it were immaculate and well-groomed. The roadway to the manor house was as straight as an arrow, lined with shrubs and trees that were all planted in neat, formal rows. The house itself was large, with three full stories of near featureless walls, except for rows of unadorned windows and a central door.

William Kirwan stepped out of the carriage as soon as it stopped and reached up so that the driver could hand him our valises.

"Follow me, gentlemen," he said to us, turning and walking toward the door of the house as he spoke.

A maid opened the door and gave a slight bow and forced smile to us as we entered. She was youngish and, like so many country girls of England, rather plain, with a moon face and eyes that bulged slightly. She was not underfed.

"Maggie," said Kirwan, "please show these gentlemen to the library. The squires are expecting them. I will let them know they have arrived."

Then, turning to us, he continued, "You will most likely be made to wait for half an hour simply as a matter of arrogance on behalf of the Germans. However, the chairs are comfortable and there are a few decent books to read. Kindly now, excuse me gentlemen, and I trust you *will* govern yourselves accordingly."

He gave a stiff bow and disappeared down a hallway that was lined with heads of various species of hunted animals. Holmes and I waited in silence in the library. I passed the time by scribbling in my notebook whilst Holmes perused the volumes and photographs on the shelves.

"Anything of interest?" I asked him, to alleviate the boredom.

"Interestingly," he replied without turning away from the shelves, "there is nothing of interest."

"Holmes," I said.

He gave a low chuckle. "Every single book is in English and all appear to have been left behind by the widow who sold the house to these fellows. There is even a set of Pope's *Homer,* complete except for the fifth volume. There is not a single volume in either French or German or whatever native tongue these fellows speak. Most former soldiers have at least a few volumes of military history that they insist on taking with them as if they were their favorite pets, but these chaps are bereft of such works. There is a small framed photograph of men in uniform, but that's all. Their military experience has been all but erased."

I returned to my notebook and he to the next wall of shelves. It was a full forty-five minutes before the door opened and two men entered. Both were very casually dressed in riding clothes and bore a distinct family resemblance to each other. The older man, the father, was well into his seventies, and the younger closer to my age. Both were tall and thin, with short, cropped blond hair and neat military mustaches. Had I not been told that they were former officers in Bismarck's army, I might well have guessed.

"Good afternoon," said the younger chap. "We welcome the esteemed Messrs. Holmes and Watson to the Hills of Lorraine. I trust your journey was a comfortable one."

I had expected to hear a German accent, but there was not a trace. Using what limited skills I had acquired in my years with Holmes, I deduced that he must have had an English governess. The Germans are rather fond of their connection to our Queen and enjoy indulging in spinsters from Oxfordshire along with shortbread and Harris tweed.

Holmes did not answer the question but spoke bluntly to the man.

"Herr Kellerman, I assume you received and read the telegram we sent you."

"Yes."

"You are aware, then, that several of your fellow officers from your time in the war have been murdered."

"Yes. We know that."

"I have good reason to believe that the murderer will soon come here and attempt to murder you in the same manner. I advise both of you to vacate this place immediately and move to a safer location. I have notified Scotland Yard of my concerns and they have agreed to provide a guarded residence in London until the murderer is apprehended."

"Really, Mister Holmes," interrupted the younger man. "You cannot expect us to go fleeing from our home every time someone tells us that there might be someone somewhere who does not like us. Really, sir, this is hardly the first time we have received threats and warnings and, I assure you, we are not cowards. Both my father and I have served with distinction in the Prussian army, where turning and running away were not options. We appreciate your apparent efforts on our behalf, however, other perspectives have come from officials in our embassy who, I assure you, have access to information far beyond that of an amateur detective."

Holmes stiffened on that one but retained his cool composure.

"I regret that I do not have the same privileged data that your embassy officials do. All I know is that five men, your former fellow officers, are now dead and I have good reason to believe that you are next on the list. I came only to apprise you of what I know and urge you to take precautions."

The younger would-be squire relaxed his expression and responded.

"We appreciate your concern for us, Mr. Holmes. It is not that we refuse to acknowledge the threat. Obviously, there is danger. But we will not run away. We have, you will be pleased to know, hired a dozen excellent men, all veterans of the Prussian army, to serve as our bodyguards and to patrol the property. They will continue to look after us until you and your friends at Scotland Yard, and all those clowns in the *gendarmes de Paris* solve this spate of crimes and catch the villain.

"Now then, gentlemen," he continued, "you have come here in good faith and we welcome you as our guests for dinner and the evening. We will not need your offers of advice after breakfast tomorrow and you will be free to return to London and your detective practice. Is that quite correct, father?"

"Ja."

The old fellow gave a shallow bow toward us and turned and departed from the room. His son followed. Once they had gone, Holmes and I found ourselves standing alone in the library looking quizzically at each other. The situation was relieved by the entrance of Kirwan who stood straight and announced, "Dinner will be served at half-past seven o'clock in the dining room. If you will follow me, I will show you to your rooms. You are free to enjoy the gardens until dinner time. This way, please gentlemen."

The rooms were clean and furnished in a modern fashion, albeit Spartan. The mattresses were thin and firm and the chairs were all upright. In a way, this was satisfying to me as it confirmed my prejudices about Germans' abhorrence of creature comforts. I had hardly sat down to add to my notes than Holmes tapped on my door.

"From my window," he said, "I can see the next house along the road. I am guessing that the owner is the one referred to by Mister Kirwan."

"The chap at odds with the Cunninghams over property?" I said.

"Exactly. And as we have two and a half hours until supper is served, I suggest that we pay him a visit and have a bit of a chat. Are you up to a stiff walk?"

"I am," I said and we walked out of the manor house and along the manicured paths, through the geometric gardens and over to the neighbor's house.

This home, while of similar size and construction to the one in which we were staying, looked somewhat different. Every wall of the house was bordered by a garden bed in which were planted a limited assortment small ornamental trees. The grounds and gardens adjacent to the drive that lead up to the door were similar in their orderliness and neat geometric design to the estate in which we were staying. The walls were painted white and the windows were unadorned with shutters, and above the front door an overly large Union Jack had been hung on a protruding flag pole. If this house could speak, I thought, it would be shouting 'Rule Britannia.'

Holmes appeared not to notice the landscaping or look of the house and was making a beeline to the front door. He gave a friendly, rhythmical knock on the door and pasted a smile on his face as it opened. The young blonde maid who answered was most assuredly not English, as no English girl engaged in service would dream of wearing a uniform that not only was suggestive of an Alpine milk maid but displayed so vast an expanse of generous bosom.

"*Guten tag*," she said pleasantly. "Please to come in. May I make announcement to *der Knappe* of our visitor?"

Holmes handed her his card and I did likewise. She glanced at them and her eyes widened.

"*Heiliger Strohsack!*" Sherlock Holmes and Doctor Watson. *Beeindruckend!*" She gave a smile and a stiff bow, turned and disappeared into the back of the house. We stood for several minutes in the entry hall glancing about at the variety of items mounted on the walls and side tables. There was a photograph of an impressive looking young man in uniform, a crucifix, some paintings in the recent European style that I considered smudged, a portrait of the Queen and, on the side table, a large pile of recent newspapers from the Continent and a large bust of Beethoven.

Holmes focused his gaze on the furnishings and photographs until his concentration was interrupted by the entrance of the master of the estate. A tall, broad-shouldered man of about fifty approached us. He was quite a handsome fellow, with a full head of bushy silver hair and attractive blue eyes.

"Well now, isn't this just the cat's pajamas!" he said in a refined Oxford accent as he approached us. "Is it possible? By the great detective Sherlock Holmes my humble home is visited, and the famous writer, Doctor Watson. Rather takes the egg on a sunny afternoon. To what do I owe this honor? Please, gentlemen, come in and be seated. Some brandy, perhaps. Or shall I have our Swiss miss organize a cup of tea? Please, do come in and yourselves make comfortable."

We entered a finely appointed front parlor and were seated.

"Permit me to introduce myself," he said. "I am Percy Sheridan, formerly of Leeds and London, and now of Surrey. But then, since you are Sherlock Holmes, you must have already known that, I make the assumption."

He laughed at his pleasantry and we exchanged a minute of idle chitchat about Holmes's reputation before Holmes cut off the exchange.

"Forgive my lack of grace," he said, "but we are not here to talk about the weather. I have a more serious concern that I must address to you."

"Jolly good, then," responded Mr. Sheridan with a smile. "Then please, proceed."

"I came to Surrey because of your neighbors, the Cunninghams."

Sheridan responded with a shrug. "You don't say, Mr. Holmes. This does not surprise me. If you told me that you had investigated them and that they were about to be arrested, thrown in prison, and hanged, I could only say that it was about time. Scoundrels, both of them. Please tell me that soon they will be arrested."

"No, I cannot tell you that. What I will tell you is that it is more likely that they will be murdered if they remain in their house."

"Indeed? Well, now, quite frankly, I must say that is jolly good news. Perhaps the world would be a better place if that were to be made to happen."

Holmes gave the fellow a bit of a look. "That is not exactly a charitable thing to say about one's neighbor."

Sheridan laughed. "It is only what I would say about *these* neighbors. And it is no more than any of their neighbors would say about them. The good yeomen of this town do not like any Johnny-come-lately outsiders, myself included, but Squire Cunningham with a passion they hate, and his son even more. If some day you find them done in, you will have no fewer than a hundred local Lushingtons to suspect, every one of them the honor claiming." He laughed again.

"Let me assist you," he continued. "A start on your list of suspects. Number one," he said, extending his thumb, "would have to be our fine local constable. Forrester's his name. The younger junior squire seduced his sister and ruined her. So he's been heard saying that he'd like to kill the blackguard. Number two," he added, extending his index finger, "would be the barkeep. His dear widowed mother was swindled by the older squire and the poor man lost his entire inheritance. And number three," he concluded, adding his middle finger, "might very well be the vicar, who has no specific complaint, but is outraged by the debauchery and misery those two have visited upon his faithful flock. There, is that enough of a start for you, Mr. Holmes?" Again, he laughed merrily.

Holmes smiled in return. "And what about you, Mr. Sheridan. Your dispute over property would give you a place on your list, would it not?"

That brought about a loud guffaw. "Aha! Our detective has been doing his homework. Jolly good. Why of course, you can add me. But in all modesty, I could not claim a post above number ten. Lawyers from both sides may be at it with both hands, but all the stake that is of me is a parcel of land, not the destruction of my honor or the theft of my inheritance. But by all means, do not leave me off your list." Again, the laughter.

Holmes did not join in the laughter or even smile. "In truth, sir, the danger is not from the local citizenry, sir. I have reason to believe that someone from the Continent may arrive and seek to do them harm."

"You don't say. The man's name, do you happen to have it? I assure you that the keys to the town he will be awarded."

We chatted for several more minutes, but it was obvious to me that Holmes had had enough of this jolly chap from the North. We excused ourselves, claiming that our dinner would be waiting and returned to The Hills of Lorraine. Holmes walked in silence, his hands thrust into the pockets of his coat and his chin nearly resting on his chest.

Our hosts did not join us for dinner and it was served by the moon-faced English maid, who did her best to be pleasant and offer some meaningless chit-chat, but Holmes was having none of it. He glowered at the schnitzel and sauerkraut that was served to him and ate the entire meal in silence.

Chapter Five
Not Wanted, So Back to 221B

The following morning the same young maid assisted us with our departure from the manor house. She appeared to be thoroughly intimidated by Sherlock Holmes but she stood beside me for a moment and spoke quietly.

"We're so sorry to see you leave us, Dr. Watson," she said. "When we saw the two of you arrive, all of the staff got our hopes up that something was about to change here. It is a terribly unhappy situation we are all in."

I smiled at her. "My dear, you will just have to wait it out for another few months, then your five years will be up and you will be free to seek another position."

"I suppose so, sir," she sighed. "But if you hear of the squires' dying from drinking poisoned tea, you can have the entire lot, all twelve of us, arrested."

For a brief second a thought flashed through my mind. Having twelve people all conspire together and jointly commit a murder would be a splendid basis for a mystery story.

I smiled again, and as I was old enough to be her father, I put my arm around her shoulder and offered some bland words of encouragement. William Kirwan loaded our valises into the carriage but did not join us on the return trip to the station. As we passed out of the gate, I noticed two large Teutonic-looking men standing guard. At the Reigate station, I saw another three of them standing and shaking hands and introducing themselves to each other. I concluded that the squires had indeed hired some of their countrymen to guard their estate.

"We have some time," said Holmes, "before the train to London departs. Let us pay a brief visit to the local constable. He's just next door."

The local constable, a friendly fellow named Stuart Forrester, welcomed us to his station. He appeared to be quite pleased to meet Sherlock Holmes but was obviously perplexed as to why Holmes would be visiting his village. Holmes explained the reasons for our visit and gave a very stern warning that a murderer would soon be making a visit to Reigate with the intent of doing in the younger Cunningham, and possibly the father as well.

"Very good, Mr. Holmes," said Constable Forrester. "But having one more person to suspect of murdering those two blackguards would extend my list to over twenty. The local folks do not like those two at all. And if a stranger comes to do the deed, I will guarantee that he will be among friends here for the rest of his life."

"So I have been led to believe," said Holmes, with a grim smile. "But please note; the person most likely to appear is not a man. It will be a young woman, and a highly attractive one at that."

Forrester raised his eyebrows. "Well now, wouldn't that just take the biscuit. You say a pretty young lass might come to Reigate and murder those scoundrels. There would be a score of young local lasses and a few widows who would nominate her for sainthood if that were to happen."

"It is not my role," said Holmes, "to render judgment on the victims. I only beseech you to be vigilant so that a crime will be prevented. May I count on you to respond accordingly?"

"Of course, you may, Mr. Holmes. I will swear on my honor that should I see a beautiful young woman in town who is unknown amongst us and who may have come with murderous intent … well … I swear that I will declare that I am too sick to continue working for the rest of the day and will be found recovering my health at the Bull's Head."

Holmes glared at the constable who met him eye to eye and said nothing.

"Very well, Constable Forrester," said Holmes. "I believe I understand what you are telling me. Good day, sir."

"Good day, Mr. Holmes, Dr. Watson. Sorry I could not be of more use to you."

For the first half hour of the return trip to Victoria, Holmes sat in silence. As we passed Croydon, he looked up at me.

"Those Prussian veterans will most likely be useless," he muttered. "She will get past the guards and kill them both within a fortnight. Mark my words. They are as good as dead."

"Is there not anything you can do to protect them?" I asked.

He shook his head. "I cannot force anyone to become my client, least of all a couple of pig-headed Germans. If I might offer you a turn of phrase for your notebook, you could say that I predicted that both of them will become eyesores."

I chuckled at Holmes's gallows humor and we continued the rest of the journey back to Baker Street in silence.

The next three days passed uneventfully. I tended to my patients whilst Holmes puttered away with his chemistry experiments and readings. It was not difficult for me to see that his mind was elsewhere and from time to time I observed him clenching his fists and shaking his head.

On the morning of the fourth day, as we sat quietly enjoying the delectable breakfast Mrs. Hudson had prepared for us, the bell sounded at the door on Baker Street. A minute later, Mrs. Hudson entered.

"It's the Inspector, Mr. Holmes. I told him you were still at your breakfast but he said he was coming up anyway. Shall I show him in?"

Holmes pushed his chair back from the table and sighed. "Yes, you may. And you may as well make him a fresh cup of tea and bring him some biscuits and jam. I suspect he has been up for several hours and will not be in a good humor."

Inspector Lestrade appeared almost immediately. As predicted by Holmes, his ferret-like face was even darker than usual.

Without bothering to rise from his chair or even look up, Holmes spoke into his tea cup.

"Good morning, Inspector. Nasty business, that, down in Surrey, what say? Got them good in the old eyeball, eh."

I was looking up at Lestrade even if Holmes was not. A flush of anger spread across his face and I heard him suck in a deep breath of self-control before speaking.

"I did not come here to endure your taunts, Holmes. I have two murders on my hands, which is bad enough, but I am informed that Sherlock Holmes met with the victims three days ago and warned the local constable that they were about to be murdered. Is that correct, Holmes?"

He sat down on the settee and folded his arms across his chest. The dutiful Mrs. Hudson handed him a cup of tea and he graciously thanked her before returning his scowl to Holmes.

"Yes, Inspector," said Holmes. "That is correct and I suspect that the murderer got clean away with the deed. Is that also correct?"

"No," said Lestrade. "That is wrong. We have him locked up behind bars already but I need a statement from you. We had to lean on the carriage driver a bit hard, but he admitted that he had heard the man-servant, a Mr. William Kirwan, say that he would like to kill the two victims, and he said so in your presence. So, I need you to corroborate. Did he say that to you, Holmes? Yes, or no?"

Holmes's mouth involuntary opened and a look of shock and dismay spread across his face.

"No, Inspector, no. You have it all wrong."

"What do you mean 'No' Holmes. Are you denying that William Kirwan said that to you? Did he or didn't he?"

"That is what he said, but he is not the murderer."

"He had," said Lestrade, "the motive, the means, and the opportunity. That is what we look for, isn't it, Holmes. You've just confirmed that he said he wanted to kill them and two days later, they're dead. Other than the simple maid, he was the only person in the house when the deaths occurred. What do you mean telling me that he's not the murderer?"

Sherlock Holmes very seldom if ever loses his composure, but I had never seen him so flustered and ill at ease as he was whilst being cross-questioned by Lestrade.

"That man … Mr. Kirwan … he is innocent. He is a good man. You have the wrong person. He could not have done it."

"It is rather obvious to me, Holmes that he most certainly *could* have done it. You're going to have to do better than that. Now, I have a statement here that says that Sherlock Holmes acknowledges hearing Mr. William Kirwan, the man-servant of the Squires Cunningham, father and son, clearly and distinctly state that he wished to kill his masters. Kindly sign it and I'll be on my way. And please thank Mrs. Hudson for the tea."

Holmes drew a deep breath and sat back in his chair. He seemed to have recovered his self-control and spoke in deliberate, measured tones to Lestrade.

"Inspector Lestrade," he said. "You and I have had our differences from time to time."

"That is an understatement, Holmes. Get on with it."

"I am, however, entirely certain that you know, beyond any doubt, that in spite of our differences, both of us have devoted our lives to the pursuit of justice."

"And I do not have time for a Sunday School lesson, Holmes."

"Very well then. I will tell you that I am entirely certain, beyond any doubt, that William Kirwan is innocent of the murder of the squires and that if he is punished for the crime, you will have sent an innocent man to the gallows."

"The evidence is all stacked up against him, Holmes. If he didn't do it, then who did?"

Holmes rose from his chair and walked over to the window, slowly lit a cigarette and took two slow drafts. Lestrade was showing signs of impatience.

"Holmes, I am getting old waiting. I have two murders to deal with and if you have evidence then I need to hear it. Now."

"Have you ever," said Holmes, speaking to the bay window and the cloudy sky beyond, "Heard the name, Annie Morrison?"

Lestrade's glare could have burned holes into Holmes's back.

"Of course, I have heard the name, Holmes. You and I are connected to the same web of rumors. Are you suggesting that this chimera of international crime, this avenging angel who has been a nightmare on the Continent and in America, but never once appeared, even in a dream, in Britain, suddenly dropped out of the sky and into Surrey, did in two squires, and then vanished? Are you taking me for such a fool as to believe that? What's next? Dracula in Derbyshire? Beelzebub in Bucks? What sort of fool do you think I am?"

Holmes turned back, came over and sat across from him. Slowly and patiently he presented the evidence he had assembled and the conclusions he had deduced so far in this gruesome case. Lestrade interrupted him rather rudely many times and cross-questioned him quite aggressively. Holmes endured the disrespect and relentlessly piled observations and deductions on top of each other until the expression on Lestrade's face softened and began to nod his head slowly. Finally, he stood up and walked slowly toward the door, but before getting there he reached into a pocket in his suit coat, extracted an envelope, and dropped into onto a side table.

"I reserved a cabin for the three of us on the noon train to

Surrey," he said. "I told Constable Forrester to disturb nothing and keep the room chilled, and that I would be there by one thirty and would be bringing Sherlock Holmes with me."

Holmes looked positively befuddled.

"I beg your pardon?" he said.

Lestrade turned back to face him. "Look here, Holmes. I was not born yesterday. I've been in this game far too long not to know the difference between an open and shut murder case, and one that is apparently open and shut and into which Sherlock Holmes has already stuck his bloody nose. As soon as I was informed that you had been poking around, I knew jolly well that there was something rotten in the state of Denmark. I'll see you at a quarter to noon on the Victoria platform. We have rooms reserved at the inn."

Holmes, irresistibly I could tell, smiled at him. "I look forward to the excursion," he said, "But you might think about Macbeth rather than Hamlet."

Lestrade gave him one last look, shook his head, and departed.

Chapter Six

The Mysterious Maiden Appears

"Would you mind, terribly," he said to me, "making alternative arrangements for your patients for the next two days? I would be most grateful for your assistance."

"I was just scribbling a note to Dr. Ansthruser, asking him to assist me. I did the same for him a fortnight ago. I am sure he will and I would not think of letting you return to Reigate without me, what with Dracula and Beelzebub and a murdering maiden on the loose."

"Splendid," he said. "And you might bring your service revolver along with you. It is always better to bring a gun if your assailant is bearing a dagger. Now then, we have a few hours before we have to be at the station, and I would like to enjoy the rest of my tea, which was so rudely interrupted by the dear Inspector."

He was positively beaming and smiling into his teacup. His entire body had been possessed with that unmistakable zeal that I have seen time and again when he sets out on a quest in pursuit of a villain whose machinations require the application of his most intense resolve and reasoning.

I smiled at him, fondly I admit, and again thanked heaven for my unique opportunity to assist him and chronicle his adventures.

Our brief moment of delightful anticipation did not last.

There was a soft knock at the door on Baker Street and Mrs. Hudson soon appeared.

"It's a young lady, Mr. Holmes. I told her that you were still at breakfast but she would not listen to me. She is terribly distraught and insists that she has been horribly wronged and that her honor is at stake, and if she cannot see you immediately she will have to throw herself into the Thames. Mind you, she is young and looks a bit the athlete and I suspect she knows how to swim. And, she is an American. Shall I send her away?"

Holmes sighed, leaned back in his chair and rolled his eyes up toward the ceiling. His weakness for members of the fair sex in distress was the chink in his armor and he gave a nod to Mrs. Hudson.

"Show her in. We have a few minutes still to spare and we may as well give her a listen. Did she give you her name?"

"Yes. She said her name was Annie Morrison."

Holmes and I stared at each other in disbelief and quickly put down our tea and rose to our feet. I had a fleeting thought that I should rush to my room and fetch my service revolver but before I could move a young woman appeared in our doorway. She was of medium stature and proportions and dressed most fashionably. Her chestnut hair was perfectly arranged on top of her head but what was striking about her was her face. She was one of the most beautiful young women I had ever seen in my entire life, anywhere on earth. Her features were obviously not those of our plain English lassies, and certainly not the rugged healthy look of a typical American girl. If anything, they were French, and her brilliant smile was utterly disarming.

"Oh my," she said with an undertone of laughter and a distinctly American accent. "I do hope I am not disturbing your two wonderful gentlemen too much? Please, allow me to give you my calling card. I specially selected it just for this morning. I do understand that Mr. Sherlock Holmes is a collector of such rare and refined instruments."

She walked directly to the coffee table, reached into her handbag and placed a small dagger on the table. I did not have a clear view of it but it was unadorned and appeared to be a narrow blade, no more than five inches in length. What was odd was the metal apparatus that extended from one side of the hilt. Affixed to it was a small hollow triangle of about a half an inch along each side.

This brazen young woman then sat down on the settee and smiled beautifully but shamelessly at Sherlock Holmes.

"My dear Mr. Holmes, I am a damsel in distress and in desperate need of your services. Shall I state my case, kind sir?"

Holmes was still standing and glaring down at her.

"I do not offer my services to paid assassins. Now, either give a reason for your presence here immediately or I shall call for the police to have to arrested."

"Oh my," she said and laughed merrily. "You do me wrong to cast me off so discourteously. But comply, I shall. In fact, kind sir, I shall give you three excellent reasons why you should refrain from calling the police."

Holmes said nothing and continued to stand and stare at her. I sat down and did the same, already, I must confess intrigued by this lovely if deadly apparition in 221B Baker Street.

"Well, Mr. Holmes, the first reason why you must not call the police is the fact that three years ago I took the gold ribbon in revolver shooting in the Rod and Gun Club of Houston, besting every one of the men who competed against me. You can read about it in the Houston Chronicle. I was listed under another name but it is all there, I assure you, sir."

Holmes countenance did not soften. "Quit wasting my time."

"Oh my, sir. You do appear to demand haste. Such a shame. Very well then, here is my second reason. In my handbag is a Colt 45 and my hand, as you can observe, is already placed inside as well. So I am sure that you, being the brilliant detective that you are, will have deduced that my hand is firmly holding my gun and that if you rush to the window to summon the police, well, I will just have to stop you in your tracks. But I swear, sir, I would only give you a very small wound in one of your legs from which you would soon recover. I would do that, sir, out of professional courtesy since I believe in my heart of hearts that you and I truly are fighting for the same army of justice and righteousness. Now, may I give you my third reason?"

"Speak," said Holmes. I could see that the cold fury had slipped away from his face.

"Because you know, and I know, and I know that you know that I know, that your brilliant mind is burning with curiosity and very eager indeed to learn what it is that moved me to such an unexpected act as to invade your presence on such a lovely spring morning. And so you cannot resist the opportunity hear me out, knowing that it may be the only chance you will ever have for such an encounter. Would I be correct in that assumption, Mr. Holmes?" Yet again, she laughed merrily and infectiously.

Holmes shook his head but did so clearly in chagrin and resignation and sat down across from the beautiful young American.

He nodded to her. "You may proceed. But I reserve the right to send you off to the gallows once you have imparted your information."

She flashed him a brilliant smile, wriggled her bosom in a contrived attempt to become more comfortable and began.

"Well now, Mr. Holmes. You know and I know that there is a good man, a fine husband and father, in Surrey named William Kirwan who has been falsely charged with the murder of those two terrible men, *Herr Kellerman vater* and *herr sohn*. And it would be a terrible injustice if the dear Mr. Kirwan had to suffer a minute more than necessary for a crime he did not commit."

She paused and looked sweetly at Holmes. He said nothing.

"And, of course, Mr. Holmes, you are convinced that the foul deed was carried out by none other than yours truly. That is what you think, is it not, Mr. Holmes?"

Again, Holmes said nothing.

"Well, sir. I will swear to you while standing on a stack of Bibles on top of my grandmother's grave, that I did no such thing. Now, do not get me wrong. I fully admit that I came to England with the intention of executing those two villains but someone somehow got to them before I did. And I assure you, sir, that had I done the deed I would not be proclaiming my innocence since I would have been paid handsomely by my current employer for carrying out such a service. But my mommy and daddy—well, in truth they were my adopted mommy and daddy—made sure that I knew that no matter how hungry or desperate I might be, I was never to take anything that did not rightfully belong to me. So my income, on which I was counting, has now vanished. Now that is bad enough, but if you insist on apprehending me then the true villain will get away scot free and neither you nor I would be very pleased with that prospect, now would we Mr. Holmes? Now, sir, will you permit me to tell you the rest of my story?"

"You may," said Holmes.

"Well now, that is real good of you, kind sir. Or perhaps it would be better if I were to drop the pretense and say, *très bien, mon confrère*. Then I will explain who I am and what has led me to seek your help."

I was startled. The Texan drawl had disappeared and in its place was a very light French accent, such as one might hear from highly educated female members of a sophisticated Parisian salon. She smiled rather seductively and continued.

"Allow me to introduce myself properly, Monsieur Holmes. My true name is not Annie Morrison. I am Jeanne d'Arc Eleanor Josephine Bastien-Lepage. I was given the name of the saintly warrior because my mother was born in Domrémy-la-Pucelle, the birthplace of the maiden saint, and she gave me that name, for which I am forever honored. I was born in the town of Saint-Avold in the region of Alsace, where I lived until I was ten years old, and since then, until four years ago, I lived in the great city of Houston, in the Republic of Texas. Recently I have lived where *le Seigneur,* in his divine wisdom, has sent me.

"I assure you, Mr. Holmes, that I am not a paid assassin, as you have called me. I am an executioner, divinely called by Almighty God, through his servant, St. Michael. I have never done any harm to anyone on earth except for the execution of those evil men who have somehow managed to escape human justice and who St. Michael has told me that I must dispatch to their well-deserved eternity in hell."

Good heavens, I thought to myself. This one truly takes the biscuit. Sitting in our rooms in Baker Street was a stunningly beautiful young woman, who was not only a ruthless murderer but nuttier than a fruitcake. I was not particularly concerned for our safety, but I was surprised to see the look on Holmes's face. He appeared not to be dismissive of this lovely but insane young woman, but to be accepting and indeed intrigued.

"I have been told," she continued, "in a vision that came to me late last night, that I must set aside my other tasks and prove the innocence of Mr. Kirwan. You, sir, I have been informed by my reliable contacts at Scotland Yard, have accepted the same assignment. As we find ourselves on the same team, so to speak, I will accompany you later today to Surrey. I will see you shortly on the platform at Victoria. Permit me to bid you *adieu* until then."

She rose and smiled again in a beguiling manner at Holmes and also at me. I was speechless from her utter audacity, but Holmes responded in a most gracious voice.

"We shall look forward to your company, Mademoiselle Bastien-Lepage. But permit me to offer one small piece of advice. If you wish to lie about having a Colt 45 in your handbag, it would be useful to carry something in it that had a similar weight, a small rock perhaps, so that your bag did not ride so lightly on your arm."

Her face registered an element of surprise, and she glanced at her purse. "Oh my," she said, the Texas accent having returned, "you truly are quite observant. I so look forward to working with you. I am sure that I will be a much improved liar as a result of our time together."

She departed and I glared at Holmes.

"You just let her walk away," I sputtered. "If she is who you say she is then she is responsible for a string of murders all across America and Europe. What are you thinking, Holmes?"

"I am thinking, my dear Watson, that I am aware of her trail of executions but I also know that not one of them to date has taken place in Great Britain or anywhere in the Empire where British law would apply. And evidence against her on the Continent or in America is no more than rumor. There are no grounds on which to arrest her."

Here he paused, and then, with a trace of a smile, he added, "And, Watson, I confess that I find her quite interesting. She is as mad as a hatter and utterly deluded, but all the same is one of the most brilliant criminal minds I have ever encountered. If my information is correct, she has dispatched up to twenty men, all of whom had highly unsavory reputations, and there is not a shred of evidence against her. Observing her for as long as I am given the opportunity will be most stimulating."

He retreated then to his bedroom, turning to me only to say, "We should depart at half-past eleven. And it might be best if you brought your service revolver along with you."

Chapter Seven
Return to Surrey After the
Murder

At ten minutes to noon, Holmes and I stood with Inspector Lestrade on the platform of Victoria Station. Lestrade was talking away about the puzzling murders but Holmes was not paying close attention. His eyes were glancing up and down the platform, clearly looking to see if the divine executioner would show up. I was ready to conclude that she had lied about meeting us when, at a minute before the train was to depart, she sauntered out of the station and appeared beside us. Lestrade gave her a most peculiar visual inspection and then gave looked at Holmes that in unspoken terms demanded an explanation.

"Inspector Lestrade," said Holmes, "allow me to introduce Miss Annie Morrison. She will be accompanying us to Reigate."

The look on Lestrade's face was one of astonishment, followed quickly by anger.

"Look here, Holmes. I have neither the time nor the patience for your games. If you have no more character than to bring along a mistress half your age on official Yard business, then I have lost whatever respect I may have had for your honor. I will see you in Reigate."

He turned on his heel and walked toward a railway cabin and closed the door rather smartly behind him.

"Oh my," sighed Miss Morrison, or whoever she was. "That policeman was rather rude to you, sir, and not at all chivalrous to a young lady." She let out a trill of laughter and added, "But I do confess that being mistaken as the mistress of the illustrious Mr. Sherlock Holmes is rather flattering. I have been called much worse in the past and expect that I shall be again in the future. It is an unexpected honor to be called upon to play such a distinguished role."

Holmes gave her an angry look but she smiled in a manner that I would have termed loving had it not come from so accomplished an actress. Holmes was disarmed and, for a passing second, I was quite sure that he blushed.

Once inside the cabin, Holmes, having recovered his composure, turned to her and said, "It will take at least an hour to get to Reigate. I believe, Miss, that you are under some degree of obligation to give a full accounting of who you are. Kindly state you case. I have no doubt that half of what you say will be falsehoods."

Again, the smile and the laugh. "How astute of you, Mr. Holmes. But do tell; which half will that be? And how will you know?"

She settled back into her seat across from us, stretched out her legs, exposing several inches of perfectly formed calf, and grinned.

"This is the account of Jeanne d'Arc Bastien-Lepage," she began, *sans* the American accent. "I am sure, Monsieur Holmes that you are aware that during the years of 1870 and 1871, there was a war fought between Prussia, or Germany as it is now called, and France. The town of Saint-Avold lies close to the German border and was quickly occupied by the invading forces of the Prussian army. Over a hundred and fifty thousand soldiers passed through our town on their way to the battle of Metz, a few kilometers to the west. But Metz held out and was besieged from August until October, when the people of the city were facing starvation and the French forces had to surrender. Our lovely, ancient town was used by the Prussian army as a center for supplying food to the troops who were fighting in Metz. Most of our food was taken during those months but that was a hardship we could have borne.

"The Prussian army was a perfectly disciplined fighting machine, the best in the world, and the officers had to obey a code of military conduct, and they had orders to leave the citizens in peace as long as the food quota was supplied and no resistance was given. My father was one of the leaders of our town and had a fine house. But he was passionately loyal to La France and organized a resistance movement, a band of *francs-tireurs,* that did whatever it could to frustrate the Prussians and help our men. There was always a danger that he would be found out. The town was full of spies. Since he was a civilian we knew that if he were caught, he would be sent to prison in Germany. But that, sir, is not what happened.

"The commanding officer of the company that occupied Saint-Avold was a man of unspeakable evil. He was not an honorable soldier, but the devil incarnate. He delighted in torture and debauchery and took every opportunity to line his own pocket by stealing from the people of the town. If they dared to object, he dealt with them in a way more cruel than can ever be imagined. Directly under his command were seven younger officers who, with one exception, followed the example of their colonel, and violated every rule of war, and did evil to any civilian they wished, beating and robbing the men, even killing them at times, and violating the women and young maidens horribly and shamelessly.

"As our town was in the border region between France and Prussia, there were many people who were loyal to France and almost as many whose allegiance fell with Prussia. Half of the population was spying on the other half. So it was not long before my father's work was revealed and our home was entered and my parents arrested. It was on the fifteenth of September in the year 1870. I ran upstairs to a closet where one of the Prussian soldiers found me. He was an honorable man and he immediately told me to stay hidden and under no circumstances to come out, no matter how horrible might be what I heard happening. He was very insistent. I could not see his face in the darkness but I could hear the fear in his voice. I was only seven years old, but I knew that I must do as he said.

"For three hours I hid in that closet and listened to the screams of my father as they tortured him and of my mother as they violated and beat her. I could also hear the screams of my little brother as they inflicted pain on him for no reason other than their wicked and perverse pleasure. The one officer, the man who had told me to hide, could be heard trying to get them to stop but he was laughed at and mocked.

"Then the screaming ended and it became silent. After waiting until darkness had fallen, I came out of hiding and found the mutilated bodies of my father, mother and little brother. I walked to the neighbor's home and asked for help. They were good people who had been friends for many years and they immediately took me in. With the best of loving intentions, they arranged to have me adopted by relatives living in America in the vain hope that a new life would help me get over my tragedy. I was sent to live in Texas. I was given an American name. It did not help. Every night of my life I see the same sight and hear the same screams as I saw that evening seventeen years ago.

"Every morning, I would rise up early and walk around the corner to the church for the early mass. I would kneel and receive the sacraments and hope that the pain would go away. But on my thirteenth birthday, I stayed behind and prayed to St. Michael, just as Joan of Arc had done when she was that age. As the church bells started ringing, I saw a bright light surrounding the saint and a voice spoke to me. It was Saint Michael, who I saw before my eyes; he was not alone, but was accompanied by many angels from Heaven. I saw them with my bodily eyes, as well as I am seeing you. At first, it appeared that his sword had left his hand and was floating down toward me. Then the sword became smaller and smaller until it was only a small dagger. And then came the voice.

"It said, 'Jeanne d'Arc, you are an instrument of divine justice and will bring God's wrath upon evil men.' In the days and weeks that followed, as I prayed for guidance, the voices came again and again, telling me that I had been called by God, just as had my namesake, to be His instrument and to be the divine executioner of those men who had done great evil but had escaped the punishment that the courts should have given them. The voices also told me that God had given me great physical beauty so that I could use it as a weapon against evil men. I kept all of these things in my heart until I was sixteen years of age and then the instruction from my voices became explicit.

"A man in Houston, where we lived, had been arrested for the murder of his wife. Everyone knew he was guilty but he was a very rich man and managed to bribe the jury and was declared innocent. St. Michael spoke to me and told me that I was to be the instrument of justice when human justice had failed. Again, the dagger that I had seen when I was thirteen appeared before me and then vanished. But I knew what I had to do. I procured a small dagger and gave my life over to the cause of justice, believing, like Queen Esther, that *if I perish, I perish.*

"The murderer was known to be a lecher and fond of dishonorable acts with attractive young women. I arranged to meet him and he immediately took me to his home, where he attempted to seduce me. When he was in a fit of passion, I executed him and sent him off to hell to be punished for his evil life. No one suspected me and the police did not try very hard to solve the case, as they were quite happy to see justice done even if it were not by the courts.

"I waited before God for my next divine mission. It came a few months later. The newspapers reported that a man in Galveston had been arrested for smuggling young Mexican men and women into Texas to work on the farms. But he treated them as slaves and on the boat from Tampico these men and women had been held in the hold for two weeks. Six of them had died. But because their deaths could not be proven to have taken place in America, he was not charged. St. Michael, spoke to me and told me that this man was guilty of murder and since human justice had failed, he must be executed. I was given this mission by the voice of the saint, so at the age of seventeen, I took the train the short distance to Galveston one Saturday morning. I was back home with my adopted family by the late afternoon, and the murderer had been dispatched to hell.

"In obedience to the voices of the saints, I carried out several more missions in Texas, but when I turned eighteen they told me that my mission was now to the world and so I departed from my home and my loving adopted family and since that day have had no home. When I hear of a great failure of justice, I ask St. Michael for the verdict of God and if it is 'guilty' I make contact through secret means with the families of the victims of the crime and inquire if they are interested in seeking justice and if they are willing to pay for it. Usually, they are. They never see my face, but they have, every one of them, compensated me for my work on behalf of divine justice.

"My greatest mission, as you may have deduced, has been the visiting of justice upon those men who murdered my family. The evil commander of the troops in Saint-Avold was Colonel Kellerman. They did great evil to many of the people of Saint-Avold and not just to my family. So the local lodge of the Masonic Order was very receptive to my offer to deliver justice and agreed to compensate me most generously for my services. I will, however, have to forego a portion of my fee since it was not I who dispatched father and son Kellerman, but some other person. I am determined to discover who this man or woman is so that together we might devote ourselves to the cause of divine justice and rid the earth of those evil men who have been able to elude the police and the courts. And that, sir, is why I have called upon you and have joined you on your quest in Surrey this afternoon."

She smiled, yet again and Holmes gave a forced smile in return.

"I assure you, Mr. Holmes, that what I have told you this afternoon is the truth. I have not lied to you."

"I have no doubt, Miss, that you believe that everything you have told me is the truth. You will forgive me if I am selective in what I choose to believe."

I also had no doubt that this young woman believed that she was speaking truthfully to us. It struck me that it was quite possible that her mind had come undone from the terrible events that happened when she was a child. It also occurred to me that everything she believed might be no more than an illusion and that she was merely a deluded American, born and raised in Texas, who quite sincerely believed herself to be someone entirely different than who she was— a latter-day Saint Joan of Arc. I was not sure if she should be committed to Broadmoor, or sent to the gallows, or considered for future beatification.

We had arrived at the Reigate Station and we disembarked from the train. The air was brisk and the sky was cloudless. I commented absently on the day, to which Holmes replied.

"The low temperature is fortunate. The local constable will have kept the windows of the bedrooms open so as to delay the decay of the bodies. That is always useful."

There were several cabs waiting and Mademoiselle Jeanne d'Arc and I took one whilst Holmes and Lestrade took the other. The young woman had said nothing more to us and neither Jeanne nor Annie spoke as we drove to the Kellerman estate, although from time to time I noticed her lips moving, as if she were carrying on a conversation with persons unknown.

A constable was posted at the gate of the Hills of Lorraine and two more stood guard at the gate of the house. Lestrade and Holmes had preceded our cab and were waiting for us to arrive. We got out and started walking towards the door, with Mademoiselle Jeanne obviously accompanying me. The Inspector made it clear that he was having none of Holmes's nonsense with a young mistress.

"Look here, Holmes," he barked.

"My dear, Inspector," said Holmes, interrupting him. "I assure you that my relationship with this young woman is entirely honorable, as is my relationship with any woman I have even known. I am not entirely certain who she is, but have concluded that she may have some useful data and insights to offer to the investigation and that she has committed no crime on British soil. Pray, kindly indulge her presence. I will vouchsafe for her behavior."

Lestrade looked directly at me, his face demanding that I confirm Holmes's assertion. "As far as I know," I said, not entirely confident in what I did or did not know, "you may rely on what Sherlock Holmes has told you."

I gave a bit of an emphatic nod to buttress my claim and the three of us followed the inspector into the house. For the next two hours, Holmes closely observed the courtyard, the entrance to the house, the bedrooms, and the bodies of the two victims. I followed him, making notes on what I could observe, with Holmes making the occasional comments to me regarding whatever matter he was observing.

When the close inspection of the house and the scenes of the murders had been concluded, Lestrade gave orders to the local policemen to have an undertaker remove the body and allow the household staff to re-enter the premises. The group of us then gathered back downstairs in the library.

"Very well, Holmes," said Lestrade. "Speak up. What have you *deduced,* as you like to call it?"

"The local police carefully followed your instructions and disturbed the site as little as possible. Kindly thank them for their diligence."

"I will do that," said Lestrade, "but I asked what you deduced, not what thank-you notes you wished to send."

"Yes, of course," said Holmes. "It was, however, most helpful that the soil in the courtyard had not been trampled. I observed several sets of footprints that were made by boots that are standard issue for policemen. There, though, one set that was different from the rest. Earlier this morning, I insisted that the murderer was a woman, the same young woman who now sits in this room. I must now withdraw that accusation. It could not have been her. The length of the stride and the depth of the indentation indicate that it was a male of average height and weight. Somewhat shorter than I am, and somewhat taller than you, Inspector. About the size of Dr. Watson."

"Well now, Holmes," said Lestrade, "that is so very helpful. I'd say about half the men in the village fit that description, the vicar, the priest, the doctor and the postmaster included. In fact, so does Mr. William Kirwan, who, by the way, does not wear police footwear. Pray, continue."

"The last victim I examined, in Strasbourg, was still wearing his evening clothes, or at least most of them, and his shoes. Both of these men were in their night clothes."

"Which tells me," said Lestrade, "that we are dealing with a patient Englishman rather than an impetuous Frenchman, or Italian, or whoever it was that did in your fellow in Alsace."

Holmes ignored the jibe and carried on. "The murderer in Europe killed her victims with a single stab of a short dagger into the brain. These men had been stabbed multiple times, again and again in the eye with a longer dagger. That was obvious from the blood that emerged from the mouth, nostrils and the other eye socket. This murderer was not at all skilled or certain of his trade. Yet there was a savagery to his actions; a rage. This man was angry but it is possible, indeed probable, that it was the first time he had killed a man in this manner."

"You do realize," said Lestrade, "that you are doing nothing at all to dissuade me from suspecting Kirwan. Right now, he fits your description to a T. He had access to the house, and the guards have sworn that they saw no one else on the grounds last night. I know you well enough, Holmes, to respect your instincts and your reasoning, but you'll have to do a lot better that what you've done to keep Mr. Kirwan off the gallows. Now, if you have nothing else to tell me, I have a job to do. Good day."

He rose and departed from the room, leaving Holmes, Miss Whoever-she-was, and me in the library. The moon-faced maid came, asked cheerfully if we wished tea, and departed. Holmes paced back and forth for several minutes and then found an appropriately styled chair that permitted him to draw his long legs up under his body, close his eyes, and contemplate. I made some notes about the case but admit that I had very grave doubts as to whether I would ever be able to put it on record as one that Holmes solved. Our young accomplice, with nothing else to do, wandered aimlessly around the library, nonchalantly examining random books and artifacts.

I knew enough not to disturb Holmes whilst he was in his state of concentration and so silence reigned for some fifteen minutes. It was interrupted by a loud and distressful cry from Mademoiselle Jeanne. Holmes's eyes popped open and he glared at her, thoroughly annoyed. I stood and walked over to where she had collapsed into a large chair. She had buried her head in her hands and was visibly sobbing. In her lap was a photograph. I took the liberty of picking it up and looking at it.

It was perfectly unremarkable. It was of seven men in military uniforms. Four were seated on a bench in a park, with three more standing behind them. The clarity of the picture was poor, but I could see that none was smiling. There was nothing else in the photo to distinguish it from the thousands that soldiers have taken of themselves whilst off-duty and enjoying an afternoon out with their comrades. Yet it had brought about an anguished response from the young woman.

Chapter Eight
Come, the Game is Afoot

It was most likely not a good idea to extend a compassionate hand to her shoulder, but my years as a doctor made such an action an instinctive response.

"What is it, Miss?" I asked. "What is this photograph of?"

I watched her clench her fists until her knuckles whitened and she struggled to gain control of herself. She raised her head, her lovely face streaked with tears.

"They were in the park," she said. "The park in Saint-Avold. The town park was behind our house; the house I grew up in as a child. You can see our home in the background, behind some of the trees."

She took a deep breath and reached for the photograph. "Here," she said, pointing at a small dark rectangle within the trees. "That is the window of my bedroom."

She stopped speaking for a full minute, then took another deep breath and continued. "That is the room I hid in when my parents and brother were killed. I have never been back to the house since that day."

The photograph was handed back to me as if it were too terrible to continue to look at. Holmes rose, came over and took it from me.

"And are these the men," he asked, "who you say visited such evil upon your family?"

Without speaking or removing her head from her hands, she nodded. "Saint Michael has said that they are."

Holmes took the photograph back to his chair, sat down, removed his glass from his pocket, and spent the next several minutes examining it. He then turned to the young woman.

"Get up!" he commanded. "If you are going to be useful to the cause of justice, you cannot indulge in whimpering and simpering."

She lifted her head. Her face betraying the shock of Holmes's rebuke. She nodded and stood.

"Come. We need to get into the village."

I was used to abrupt changes in Holmes's behavior. Inevitably it gave evidence of his having come to some insight in a case, but my curiosity could not be held back.

"Might I be so bold as to ask why?" I said.

"Because the murderer is most likely sitting in the pub enjoying his supper. With luck, Lestrade will be there as well."

The cab that had brought us to the Cunningham's estate was waiting for us and we quickly climbed in.

"The Bull's Head," shouted Holmes to the driver. "And quickly."

The old pub on the High Street was somewhat crowded with men and the occasional woman having a pint before supper or already digging into their steak and kidney pies. As I surveyed the patrons, I observed several of the chaps we had already met during our visits to Reigate as well as a couple of the recently hired German guards who would soon, I surmised, have to seek alternative employment given that they supremely failed in the job of protecting the squires.

I could see that Holmes was also looking around the room and his eyes settled on the far corner.

"Come, time to corner the prey," he said, and walked quickly toward a table at which only one man was sitting.

"Would you mind awfully, Mr. Sheridan, if we joined you at your table? This place is getting rather busy, is it not?"

Percy Sheridan looked up at Sherlock Holmes and smiled. His glance then went to me and then to Mademoiselle Jeanne. She gave him one of her radiant smiles and sat down.

"You have not met our young assistant," said Holmes. "Permit me to introduce our assistant, Mademoiselle Jeanne d'Arc Bastien-Lepage."

It was only a passing second, but a look of surprise mixed with fear passed over Sheridan's countenance as he observed her. He quickly recovered.

"It is a pleasure to meet you," said Sheridan.

"*Enchantée, monsieur*," came the reply.

Mr. Sheridan called the waiter over and asked for two beers for the gentlemen and a shandy for the lady.

"I assume," he said, "that you have returned to Reigate to investigate the murder of the squires. Nasty business, that, eh what?"

"Yes," said Holmes, "really quite shocking. Very confusing, wouldn't you say? I hardly know where to start. So I have no choice but to ask questions of everyone and try to put some sort of theory together."

"I suppose," said Sheridan, "that is what detectives must do."

"Yes, I suppose it is. And seeing as we are sitting here, would you mind awfully if I were to start with you?"

"Me? Well, no, not at all. I fear I may not be of much use to you, but seeing as you are sitting here anyway, then you may as well get me out of the way and off the list. What would you like to know?"

"Nothing too complicated to start with," said Holmes. "Perhaps you could explain to me how it was that you managed to get past the guards, enter the house, stab two men to death and leave again without being detected. Would you mind?"

Sheridan's face went blank. For several seconds he glared at Holmes, and then his glance traveled around the room and finally he gazed up at the ceiling. He gave a very small nod.

"Jolly well done, Mr. Holmes. Your reputation is no doubt well-deserved. But I will only respond to your question if you agree to respond to mine. How did you come to your conclusion? I would be interested in knowing."

"I will give a full answer to your question," said Holmes. "But first, how did you get past the guards?"

"It was a trifle. I became one of them. They were all still arriving and had not even finished introducing themselves to each other. I donned my old uniform and joined them. As you have likely deduced, I speak native German and told them that I had been assigned to guard the back entrance to the house. Now they have been dismissed. I would be surprised if any of them guessed for even a second that my intent was the opposite of theirs."

I observed Holmes give a small shake to his head. Not that he doubted the truth of what he was being told, but that he never ceased to wonder at the gullibility of the members of the human race.

"And now your response to my question, Mr. Holmes," said Sheridan.

"To your credit, sir, you were somewhat more astute that those who employed the guards. What revealed your identity was, in order: First, you had recently had your gardens replanted, but without a single rose bush; something no true Englishman would ever do. And no Englishman from Leeds would ever hire Brunhilde as a housekeeper and have her prepare strudel. Your accent betrays not a single trace of the North, something that even decades in Oxford cannot erase. You speak the English of a Junker who was raised by an English governess, although you, like all native German speakers, are so discourteous to your verbs, depositing far too many of them at the end of your sentences. An Englishman does not give a digital indication of his counting by beginning with his thumb. All of these observations make it obvious that you were not who you claimed to be. The final revelation was one for which I cannot take complete credit. Miss Bastien-Lepage brought to my attention a photograph of father and son Kellerman and some other Prussian army officers. You were not in that photograph, but in the small portrait of yourself which you display and I observed in your hallway—the one of you as a dashing young Prussian captain; one that you must find quite pleasing to look upon—you were standing in the same park as your fellow officers. There was no printing on the photographs to indicate that date and location, and the insignia on the uniforms was not easy to discern. But on close inspection, it could be seen that the uniforms were of the exact same style and cut and had identical markings. You were not only a fellow member of the Prussian army as the Kellermans, you were in the same company and the same unit. I do not know what your motive was. Revenge of some sort stemming from events that took place over a decade ago, perhaps. Nor have I discerned why you chose to take the actions you did last night. You must know that you are now on your way to the gallows, regardless of how much the Kellermans deserved to be punished. So, perhaps you will explain. And, whilst you are doing so, perhaps you could tell us just who you are."

Up to this point, the man, whoever he was, could simply have denied all of Holmes's accusations. I was bewildered as to why he had not done so. Now Holmes was asking him to incriminate himself whilst I recorded his words. I fully expected that the man would get up and walk away, knowing that there were no grounds on which to detain him. And yet, he did not move. He looked again up to the ceiling, gave a small nod, and continued.

"My name, sir, is Maxim von Witzleben. I am a member of a noble Prussian family that has a proud history of military service for the past three hundred years. As a young man, following my graduation from one of the finest gymnasia in Saarbrücken, I began my military service in the Prussian army, as my *Vater* and *Großvater* had done before me. To the rank of *Kapitän* and then *Zugführer* I was quickly promoted was honored to lead a *Zug* of fine men into the war with France. I served under Colonel Kellerman. Of all the soldiers I have even known, he was the most disgraceful and gave himself over to every form of evil, cruelty, and extortion. It is terrible to have to admit it, but several of my fellow officers went along with his vile activities. I refused to lower myself to their level and was ostracized for so doing. During the siege of Metz, our units were responsible for the provisioning of the troops and were we stationed in the village of

Saint-Avold, where we organized the supply of food and ammunition so that the siege could carry on until we were victorious. It was during that time that the most terrible night of my life was experienced. It was the night of September 15 in the year 1870."

Here he stopped his account to Holmes and turned and looked directly at Jeanne d'Arc Bastien-Lepage and spoke quietly to her.

"Vite, ma petite. Vite, vite. Cache toi, immédiatement. Outre le fait de quoi que vous entendez, ne bougez surtout pas. Me compendez-vous? Me compendez-vous?"

She gasped and for several seconds said nothing. Then she whispered, "C'était vous."

"Oui, ma petite, c'était moi. Forgive me, mademoiselle. Please. I should have stopped them. I should have taken out my gun and shot them to make them stop. Had I been a better man I would have done so. I am sorry."

"There is nothing to forgive," she said. "You did the best you could. Because of you, I am alive."

Her voice was no more than a whisper and the blood had drained from her face.

"Tell these men, tell them what happened. They think I am crazy. They think I have imagined what happened. Tell them what happened."

Over the next ten minutes, Maxim von Witzleban described in dreadful detail the gruesome and horrible events that took place in the Bastien-Lepage home seventeen years earlier. The details of what he recounted are far too inhuman and depraved to be recorded in this story. Suffice it to say, I, who had been a soldier myself, could not believe that any soldier, serving under any flag, could do what these men had done.

As he spoke, I looked over at Jeanne d'Arc. She was as pale as a ghost and appeared to have entered a trance-like state. Her face was completely blank and I realized that although she had heard what had taken place in her home and listened to the torture of her parents, she had not observed it with her eyes. Now, in her mind, these events were coming to life. She had come out of her safe hiding place in her closet and was in the room with her family, watching them die.

"The events of that night," said Maxim, "could not remain a secret. The truth will out. An account eventually made it all the way to the Chancellor. A secret tribunal was ordered. All who were present were found guilty of cowardly and unlawful conduct and dismissed from the Prussian army. We should have been brought before a firing squad and executed. But the war had just ended and the victory over the French was being celebrated. The noble and heroic Prussian army was being hailed as the finest in the world. All of Germany was coming together to form one great country. Had our case become public, it would have spoiled the parade. So we were treated leniently and merely dismissed in disgrace.

"I defended myself, claiming that I had not participated, but the judges ruled, quite fairly, that I should have done more to stop the crimes as they were being committed, and that I should have informed our superior officers immediately afterward, which I failed to do. So I was thrown out of the army, a humiliation to my family. Generations of the von Witzleban family had served with distinction and I alone had brought shame. But I was fortunate. My family is well-to-do and I have an income from our properties. The other officers who were present that night somehow held on to their ill-gotten gains and have prospered.

"I vowed that I would wreak revenge on the others and bring to them the justice that they had escaped. But the days passed, and the days became weeks, and then years and the horrors of that night faded. I kept telling myself again and again that I had to do something, but I did nothing. The Kellermans ran off to England, others left Germany and lived in France, others yet changed their names and led prosperous lives in Strasbourg, Bonn, and Berlin. For a decade I did nothing. Then, last year, my life changed and I set out on a path of action that culminated in my actions last night."

Here he paused and took a small sip of his ale. Holmes continued to observe him intensely. Jeanne d'Arc sat stone cold motionless, still in her trance. I gave in to my curiosity.

"Very well, sir. What happened?"

"You are a doctor, ja? Reach your hand up and gently touch the side of my head. Just here, behind my temple."

I did as requested and immediately recoiled.

"Merciful heavens. You have an enormous aneurism. If that were to burst, you would be dead in seconds."

"That, sir, is what my doctors told me as well. Just about nine months ago, it appeared. I was told that it could not be operated on and that I had, at most, a year to live. There is, as your English writer has said, nothing that so concentrates a man's mind as knowing he is about to die. It was bad enough for me that I had to stand before a panel of military judges and be found wanting. I did not want a repeat performance before Almighty God before being sent off into eternity. So I determined that I must set my affairs in order and must undertake to do what I should have done seventeen years ago. I needed to bring divine execution to the leaders of our evil band of officers. I needed to execute the Kellermans."

"I should have done the deed immediately but there was a part of me, my pride I admit, that wanted to torture the two villains with having to deal with me every day, knowing that I was giving news of their horrid pasts to the villagers and letting them be faced every day with the opprobrium of their neighbors. So I purchased the estate adjacent to theirs. They thought they would divert my efforts with a lawsuit over property, but I am not a poor man and I merely hired more expensive London lawyers than they did and frustrated their efforts."

"You have owned your property now for over six months," said Holmes. "What took you so long?"

"Procrastination, indecision, perhaps even cowardice. Deciding to commit a double murder is not a decision to make quickly. So those weaknesses combined with some affairs I had to complete. I suggest that tomorrow you inquire at the offices of Wyatt Curtis, Solicitor if you wish to know more precisely what I have been up to on that score."

"Then why last night?"

"Because of you, Mr. Holmes."

Holmes said nothing but it was obvious that he was not pleased with that answer.

"You sent a warning to the Kellermans. A village has as many spies as does Alsace, especially when the villagers are united in a common cause of hatred of their would-be squires. The telegraph office duly passed along the news. Then you showed up and personally warned them. I knew that they were arrogant and stubborn but they were not stupid. I knew that if they were convinced that danger had come too close, they would disappear. I also observed the arrival of their imperial guard of former Prussian soldiers. Those soldiers are not incompetent. It would be only a day or two before they organized themselves and began to provide impenetrable protection. Had I waited even until today, it might have been too late and my plodding efforts would have been in vain. So I thank you, Mr. Holmes."

"Then why go to the bother of stabbing them in their sleep. You could just as easily have shot them with a rifle as they walked on the property. I am sure you have one, a Mauser most likely, and you know how to use it effectively."

"Quite correct. But I had read the accounts in the newspapers from France and Germany of the murders of the other members of the evil band of officers. Copying the method of the fellow who was doing them in, one of the local masons, I assumed, might keep you and Scotland Yard off my scent. It occurred to me that I might be able to die in bed and not in a prison cell. It seemed like a good idea at the time, until they went and arrested poor Mr. Kirwan. I was terribly upset by that news and immediately wrote out a complete confession. It is in my box at my solicitor's office. You can read it at your leisure. There is really no need for me to tell you anything else. You have all the information you need."

"Yes. I do. So you will kindly excuse me whilst I track down Inspector Lestrade and turn you over to him. I fear your wish to die in your bed and not a prison cell will not be granted."

"Ah, just one moment, if you will, please Mr. Holmes."

He then turned and spoke in a strong voice to Jeanne d'Arc.

"Mademoiselle Jeanne d'Arc Bastien-Lepage. Let my final words be a plea again for your forgiveness. May God grant you mercy and heal your pain."

The young woman startled. Her blank eyes came back to life and she nodded in response.

"And may He be merciful to you as well, sir. I forgive you and my saint has told me that Our Father will also."

"Merci, mademoiselle. And now, gentlemen," he said, turning to Holmes and me, "I pray that you also will forgive me if I do not accompany you to the police station. I have no desire to spend a single night in a jail cell. And please extend my apologies to my friend, the publican, for any inconvenience I cause him. And do not forget to visit the local solicitor"

He smiled serenely at each of us in turn and then, suddenly and forcefully, he struck the heel of his right hand against the side of his head.

"No!" I involuntarily shouted.

"*Ja, und Auf Wiedersehen.*" His eyes blinked several times, then they closed. His head slumped forward and his chin rested on his cravat.

For several seconds the three of us sat in stunned silence. Then Miss Bastien-Lepage rose from her chair and walked over to Maxim von Witzleban, leaned down and planted a light kiss on is cheek. "Rest in peace, *mon capitaine*. Saint Michael told me he is waiting for you."

Chapter Nine
Where There is a Will

William Kirwan was released from police custody later that evening. The following morning, Holmes, Lestrade and I paid a visit to the offices of Mr. Wyatt Curtis, the local barrister. Jeanne d'Arc accompanied us but maintained a trance-like silence.

"Please, gentlemen and lady," said the barrister. "Do come in and be seated. And do excuse me if I seem somewhat distracted. The events of the past few days in the town have been frightfully disturbing. For ten years nothing particularly untoward took place and now were are invaded by a famous detective, Scotland Yard, and German war veterans and three men die tragically. It is a bit of a bother to our equilibrium. But enough of that, how may I be of assistance to you? I assume you are interested in the last wills and testaments recently filed by both Squires Cunningham and by Mr. Sheridan. Which one do you wish to see first?"

Not expecting this question, none of us immediately replied.

"All three," said Lestrade. "Let's have a look at them."

"Of course, Inspector. I have all three on my desk ready for you. It may come as a surprise to you to learn that neither the Cunninghams nor Mr. Sheridan were living under their legal names. The father and son are actually named Kellerman, and Mr. Sheridan was a German aristocrat, a von Witzleban."

"We were aware of that," said Holmes.

"Ah, yes. Of course. I should have expected that a Scotland Yard inspector and our famous detective had done their homework. Yes, of course. Very well. Here they are."

He handed them over to Lestrade who in turn kept one and handed the other two over to Holmes and me. As we were sitting beside each other it was easy to glance at what the other was looking at as well as the document in our own hand. Within a few seconds, Holmes, Lestrade and I all looked up from the documents and exchanged glances with each other.

"These wills have been written in the same hand," said Holmes.

"Yes, that is obvious, isn't it?" said the solicitor. "But it is not surprising. They were neighbors and appear to have hired the same secretary. Quite practical. The wills are quite straightforward. The younger squire was the only son of the older man. Neither he nor Mr. Sheridan had any issue and no other kin are named. The only unusual paragraphs are the specific and residual bequests. You can read them in section eighteen beginning on the fifth page. But allow me to summarize the for you."

"Go ahead," said Lestrade.

"Obviously there was a closer connection between the men than we local townspeople were aware of. Both estates have very considerable assets. There are many securities listed as well as the real properties here in Reigate, which were held free and clear of any liens or mortgages. Oddly, Mr. Sheridan leaves his entire estate to the church of St. Michael in the village of Saint-Avold in Alsace with instructions that the funds be used for the support of any local families still impoverished following the last war. Both of the Cunninghams leave the residuals to the same church with the identical instruction. However, the older Cunninghams makes several specific bequests to a short list of widows here in Reigate, and the younger has a similar list of funds to be given to five local spinsters. It is unusual, but it is all in order."

I did not have to be Sherlock Holmes to know immediately that the wills of the squires were blatant forgeries. Even my untrained eye could see the distinct similarity between the signature of Maxim von Witzleban and the handwriting of the body of the wills.

"Did you," asked Lestrade, "personally witness the signing of these documents?"

"Me? No," said the solicitor. "But they were witnessed by the postmaster, the vicar, and the constable. Their signatures appear on the final page. So there is no question that they are legitimate."

Mr. Wyatt Curtis looked at us, utterly stone-faced. It was clear to all present that the documents we were looking at were fraudulent and I waited for Holmes or Lestrade to say something.

"Very well, then," said Lestrade. "if they have reliable witnesses, then they should be put to effect as expeditiously as possible. You would agree, would you not, Holmes?"

"I would agree," Holmes replied.

"Excellent," said Lestrade. "And who are the executors?"

"Mr. William Kirwan," said the solicitor, "is named by all three parties. An excellent choice, I must say. Terrible mix-up he went through but that is all behind him now. He will do a capital job disbursing the funds as directed and winding up the affairs of the estates."

"I have no doubt he will," said Holmes. "He is a good man."

Lestrade departed to the train station without so much as bidding us a good day. Holmes, Jeanne d'Arc and I returned to the inn and sat down for a refreshing round of morning tea.

"Well, now, mademoiselle," I said. "What now are your plans? I hope they do not involve any more executions, deserved or otherwise."

She beamed a radiant smile at me and then replied in her broad Texan accent.

"Oh my, Doctor Watson. Why, I do believe that your Mademoiselle Jeanne d'Arc has departed. She must have gotten on the train with the terribly unpleasant policeman."

"Did she now? Well then, Miss Annie, what are *your* plans?"

"Oh my, Doctor Watson. I do believe that my gallivanting around the earth is over and done and I shall return to Houston and settle down. I will just have to find me an upright, fine young eligible gentleman with excellent prospects and a rich daddy and see to it that he marries me. I do not fancy living on a ranch with a thousand cows, but I reckon that a railway or a mining tycoon with a lovely home in the city would suit me real fine. Don't you agree, Doctor."

I laughed out loud. "I believe, miss, that you have to find that man first. The competition is quite stiff on the frontier."

"Oh my goodness gracious, doctor. That will not be at all

difficult. Men really are such simple creatures. All a gal needs to do is make the poor fools feel utterly wonderful about *themselves* when they are with you and they will never leave you. I shall send you a wedding invitation within six months. Mark my words," She laughed loudly and infectiously.

"Young lady," said Holmes. "I may not be able to fault you for your past actions, but I would hope that you would have sufficient integrity to warn whoever you plan to marry that your mind is unstable and that you are prone to hearing voices instructing you to engage in violent deeds."

The smile vanished from her face and she looked directly at Sherlock Holmes

"Yesterday, sir, when poor Mr. Sheridan was telling you about what took place seventeen years ago, the voices inside my head were screaming until I thought my head would burst. But then they went silent. This morning I woke up and I knew that I had passed the first night in a decade in which no voice spoke to me. When I looked in the mirror, the only person who was there was Annie Morrison of Houston. Mademoiselle Jeanne d'Arc had departed. St. Michael has returned to heaven. He is no longer with me."

"Has he now? And your voices?"

"Mr. Holmes, my voices are gone."

Historical and Other Notes

The primary historical background to this story is the war between France and Germany – the Franco-Prussian War – of 1870-1871. Historians debate as to what started it. Some claim it was French foolishness, others suggest that Bismarck deliberately enticed them into a war so that he could use it as a pretext for uniting the independent German states. The Prussian army, reputed to be the best fighting machine in the world at the time, trounced the French and ended up annexing the French provinces of Alsace and Lorraine.

Metz is one of the major towns in Alsace. It was attacked by the Prussian troops early in the war, but held out for several months before surrendering, an event known as the siege of Metz. Saint-Avold is a lovely historical town in Alsace, very close to the German border. It was one of the first places in France that was occupied by the Prussian troops. Other towns and cities, including Paris, endured long sieges, resulting in high numbers of civilian deaths. An estimated 750,000 deaths, combined military and civilian, are attributed to the war.

Although the war was shorter and more contained than the world wars of the twentieth century, it was a very significant historical event for several reasons:

It demonstrated that a conscript army (the Prussians), supported by highly superior preparation and logistics, could defeat a professional army that had better arms (the French);

It was one of the first times that the Red Cross played an extensive role in the treatment of the wounded and in attempts to enforce some degree of agreed upon rules of warfare. These would later be codified into a re-draft of the Geneva Conventions;

Informal guerilla resistance units were organized by the occupied

French and were somewhat effective in asymmetrical warfare. Violent and brutal reprisals against civilians were launched in response to resistance actions;

The defeat of the French and the fall of the Second Republic led to the short-lived Paris Commune. The iconic status of the Commune and the bloody crushing by the national government became seminal events in the development of world Communism;

The annexation of Alsace and Lorraine by Germany made certain that animosity between the French and Germans would continue for decades after the end of the war. It led, in part, to the chain of events that culminated in World War I;

It was the first war that was followed by the 'cult of the war dead' wherein soldiers who died in battle were buried in special cemeteries, cenotaphs erected, and remembrance ceremonies instituted.

Alsace and Lorraine remained under German control until the end of World War I. They were occupied again under Hitler and formally annexed in 1941. Over 140,000 Alsatian and Mosellian men were conscripted in the German armed forces. The territories were returned to France in 1945.

About the Author

In May of 2014 the Sherlock Holmes Society of Canada – better known as The Bootmakers (www.torontobootmakers.com) – announced a contest for a new Sherlock Holmes story. Although he had no experience writing fiction, the author submitted a short Sherlock Holmes mystery and was blessed to be declared one of the winners. Thus inspired, he has continued to write new Sherlock Holmes Mysteries since and is on a mission to write a new story as a tribute to each of the sixty stories in the original Canon. He currently writes from Toronto, the Okanagan, and Manhattan.

More Historical Mysteries
by Craig Stephen Copland

www.SherlockHolmesMystery.com

Studying Scarlet. Starlet O'Halloran has arrived in London looking for her long lost husband, Brett. She and Momma come to 221B Baker Street seeking the help of Sherlock Holmes. Three men have already been murdered, garroted, by an evil conspiracy. Unexpected events unfold and together Sherlock Holmes, Dr. Watson, Starlet, Brett, and two new members of the clan have to vanquish a band of murderous anarchists, rescue the King and save the British Empire. This is an unauthorized parody, inspired by Arthur Conan Doyle's *A Study in Scarlet* and Margaret Mitchell's *Gone with the Wind*.

A Case of Identity Theft. It is the fall of 1888 and Jack the Ripper is terrorizing London. The national Rugby Union team has just returned from New Zealand and Australia. A young married couple is found, minus their heads. They were both on the team tour. Another young couple is missing and in peril. Sherlock Holmes, Dr. Watson, the couple's mothers, and Mycroft must join forces to find the murderer before he kills again and makes off with half a million pounds. The novella is inspired by the original story by Arthur Conan Doyle, *A Case of Identity*. It will appeal both to devoted fans of Sherlock Holmes, as well as to those who love the great game of rugby.

The Adventure of the Spectred Bat.

A beautiful young woman, just weeks away from giving birth, arrives at Baker Street in the middle of the night. Her sister was attacked by a bat and died and now it is attacking her. Could it be a vampire sent by the local band of Gypsies? Sherlock Holmes and Dr. Watson are called upon to investigate. The step-father, the local Gypsies, and the furious future mother-in-law are all suspects. And was it really a vampire in the shape of a bat that took the young mother-to-be's life? This adventure takes the world's favorite detective away from London to Surrey, and then north to the lovely but deadly Lake District. The story was inspired by the original Sherlock Holmes story, *The Adventure of the Speckled Band* and like the original, leaves the mind wondering and the heart racing.

The Adventure of the Engineer's Mom.

A brilliant young Cambridge University engineer is carrying out secret research for the Admiralty. It will lead to the building of the world's most powerful battleship, The Dreadnaught. His adventuress mother is kidnapped and having been spurned by Scotland Yard he seeks the help of Sherlock Holmes. Was she taken by German spies, or an underhanded student, or by someone else? Whoever it was is prepared to commit cold-blooded murder to get what they want. Holmes and Watson have help from an unexpected source – the engineer's mom herself. This new mystery is inspired by the original Sherlock Holmes story – *The Engineer's Thumb*.

The Adventure of the Notable Bachelorette.

A snobbish and obnoxious nobleman enters 221B Baker Street demanding the help of Sherlock Holmes in finding his much younger wife – a beautiful and spirited American from the West. Three days later the wife is accused of a vile crime. Now she comes to Sherlock Holmes seeking his help to prove her innocence so she can avoid the gallows. Neither noble husband nor wife have been playing by the rules of Victorian moral behavior. So who did it? The wife? The mistress? The younger brother? Someone unknown? Fans of Sherlock Holmes will enjoy this mystery, set in London during the last years of the nineteenth century, and written in the same voice as the beloved stories of the original canon. This new mystery was inspired by the original Sherlock Holmes story, *The Adventure of the Noble Bachelor.*

The Bald-Headed Trust.

Watson insists on taking Sherlock Holmes on a short vacation to the seaside in Plymouth. No sooner has Holmes arrived than he is needed to solve a double murder and prevent a massive fraud diabolically designed by the evil Professor himself.

Moriarty has found a way to deprive the financial world of millions of pounds without their ever knowing that they have been robbed. Who knew that a family of devout conservative churchgoers could come to the aid of Sherlock Holmes and bring enormous grief to evil doers? The story is inspired by *The Red-Headed League.*

The Hudson Valley Mystery. A young man in New York went mad and murdered his father. Or so say the local police and doctors.

His mother believes he is innocent and knows he is not crazy. She appeals to Sherlock Holmes and, together with Dr. and Mrs. Watson, he crosses the Atlantic to help this client in need. Once there they must duel with the villains of Tammany Hall and with the specter of the legendary headless horseman. This new Sherlock Holmes mystery was inspired by *The Boscombe Valley Mystery.*

The Sign of the Third. Fifteen hundred years ago the courageous Princess Hemamali smuggled the sacred tooth of the Buddha into Ceylon. Since that time it has never left the Temple of the Tooth in Kandy, where it has been guarded and worshiped by the faithful. Now, for the first time, it is being brought to London to be part of a magnificent exhibit at the British Museum. But what if something were to happen to it? It would be a disaster for the British Empire. Sherlock Holmes, Dr. Watson, and even Mycroft Holmes are called upon to prevent such a crisis. Will they prevail? What is about to happen to Dr. John Watson? And who is this mysterious young Irregular they call The Injin? This novella is inspired by the Sherlock Holmes mystery, *The Sign of the Four.*

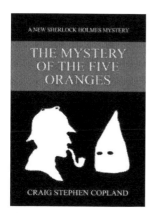

The Mystery of the Five Oranges.

On a miserable rainy evening, a desperate father enters 221B Baker Street. His daughter has been kidnapped and spirited off the North America. The evil network who have taken her has spies everywhere. If he goes to Scotland Yard, they will kill her. There is only one hope – Sherlock Holmes. Holmes and Watson sail to a small corner of Canada, Prince Edward Island, in search of the girl. They find themselves fighting one of the most powerful and malicious organizations on earth – the Ku Klux Klan. Sherlockians will enjoy this new adventure of the world's most famous detective, inspired by the original story of *The Five Orange Pips*. And those who love *Anne of Green Gab*les will thrill to see her recruited by Holmes and Watson to help in the defeat of crime.

The Adventure of the Blue Belt Buckle

A young street urchin, one of the Baker Street Irregulars, discovers a man's belt and buckle under a bush in Hyde Park. The buckle is unique and stunning, gleaming turquoise stones set in exquisitely carved silver; a masterpiece from the native American west. A body is found in a hotel room in Mayfair. Scotland Yard seeks the help of Sherlock Holmes in solving the murder. The Queen's Diamond Jubilee, to be held in just a few months, could be ruined. Sherlock Holmes, Dr. Watson, Scotland Yard, the Home Office and even Her Majesty all team up to prevent a crime of unspeakable dimensions. A new mystery inspired by *The Blue Carbuncle*.

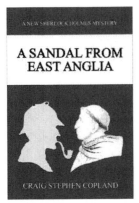

A Sandal from East Anglia.

Archeological excavations at the ruined Abbey of St. Edmund unearth a sealed canister. In it is a document that has the potential to change the course of the British Empire and all of Christendom. There are some evil young men who are prepared to rob, and beat and even commit murder to keep its contents from ever becoming known. There is a strikingly beautiful young Sister, with a curious double life, who is determined to use the document to improve the lives of women throughout the world. The mystery is inspired by the original Sherlock Holmes story, A Scandal in Bohemia. Fans of Sherlock Holmes will enjoy a new story that maintains all the loved and familiar characters and settings of Victorian England.

The Man Who Was Twisted But Hip.

It is 1897 and France is torn apart by The Dreyfus Affair. Westminster needs help from Sherlock Holmes to make sure that the evil tide of anti-Semitism that has engulfed France will not spread. A young officer in the Foreign Office suddenly resigns from his post and enters the theater. His wife calls for help from Sherlock Holmes. The evil professor is up to something, and it could have terrible consequences for the young couple and all of Europe. Sherlock and Watson run all over London and Paris solving the puzzle and seeking to thwart Moriarty. This new mystery is inspired by the original story, *The Man with the Twisted Lip*, as well as by the great classic by Victor Hugo, *The Hunchback of Notre Dame.*

The Adventure of the Coiffured Bitches. A beautiful young woman will soon inherit a lot of money. She disappears. Her little brother is convinced that she has become a zombie, living and not living in the graveyard of the ruined old church. Another young woman - flirtatious, independent, lovely - agrees to be the nurse to the little brother. She finds out far too much and, in desperation seeks help from Sherlock Holmes, the man she also adores. Sherlock Holmes, Dr. Watson and Miss Violet Hunter must solve the mystery of the coiffured bitches, avoid the massive mastiff that could tear their throats, and protect the boy. The story is inspired by the original Conan Doyle *The Adventure of the Copper Beeches.*

The Adventure of the Beryl Anarchists. A deeply distressed banker enters 221B Baker St. His safe has been robbed and he is certain that his motorcycle-riding sons have betrayed him. Highly incriminating and embarrassing records of the financial and personal affairs of England's nobility are now in the hands of blackmailers - the Beryl Anarchists - all passionately involved in the craze of motorcycle riding, and in ruthless criminal pursuits. And then a young girl is murdered. Holmes and Watson must find the real culprits and stop them before more crimes are committed - too horrendous to be imagined. This new mystery was inspired by *The Adventure of the Beryl Coronet* and borrows the setting and some of the characters.

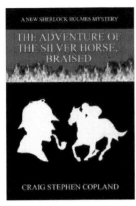

The Silver Horse, Braised. The greatest horse race of the century, with the best five-year-olds of England running against the best of America, will take place in a week at Epsom Downs. Millions have been bet on the winners. Owners, jockeys, grooms, and gamblers from across England arrive. So too do a host of colorful characters from the racetracks of America. The race is run and an incredible white horse emerges as the winner by over twenty-five lengths. Celebrations are in order and good times are had. And that night disaster strikes. More deaths, of both men and beasts, take place. Holmes identifies several suspects and then, to his great disappointment and frustration, he fails to prove that any of them committed the crime. Until… This completely original mystery is a tribute to the original Sherlock Holmes story, *Silver Blaze*. It also borrows from the great racetrack stories of Damon Runyon.

Sherlock and Barack. This is NOT a new Sherlock Holmes Mystery. It is a Sherlockian research paper seeking answers to some very serious questions. Why did Barack Obama win in November 2012? Why did Mitt Romney lose? Pundits and political scientists have offered countless reasons. This book reveals the truth - The Sherlock Holmes Factor. Had it not been for Sherlock Holmes, Mitt Romney would be president. This study is the first entry by Sherlockian Craig Stephen Copland into the Grand Game of amateur analysis of the canon of Sherlock Holmes stories, and their effect on western civilization

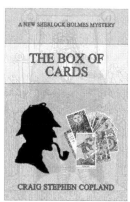

The Box of Cards. Two teenagers, a brother and a sister from a strict religious family disappear. The parents are alarmed but Scotland Yard says they are just off sowing their wild oats. A horrific, gruesome package arrives in the post and it becomes clear that a terrible crime is in process. Sherlock Holmes is called in to help. Passions and hatred going back many years are revealed. Holmes, Watson, and Lestrade must act quickly before young lives are lost. This mystery, set in London in 1905, is inspired by the original Sherlock Holmes story, "The Cardboard Box," one of the darkest and most gruesome of the original Canon. If you enjoy the mysteries of Sherlock Holmes, you will again be treated to watching your hero untangle the web of evil and bring justice to all involved.

The Yellow Farce. It is the spring of 1906. Sherlock Holmes is sent by his brother, Mycroft, to Japan. The war between Russia and Japan is raging. Alliances between countries in these years before World War I are fragile and any misstep could plunge the world into Armageddon. The Empire is officially neutral but an American diplomat has been murdered and a British one has disappeared. The wife of the British ambassador is suspected of being a Russian agent. Join Holmes and Watson as they travel around the world to Japan. Once there, they encounter an inscrutable culture, have to solve the mystery, and maybe even save the life of the Emperor. It's a fun read and is inspired by the original Sherlock Holmes story, *The Yellow Face.*

The Three Rhodes Not Taken. Oxford University is famous throughout the world for its splendid architecture, lovely manicured lawns and gardens, and passionate pursuit of research, teaching and learning. But it turns out to be at the center of a case involving fraud, theft, treachery, and, maybe, murder. The Rhodes Scholarship has been recently established and is seen at one of the greatest prizes available to young men throughout the Empire. So much so that some men are prepared to lie, steal, slander, and, maybe murder, in the pursuit of it. Sherlock Holmes is called upon to track down a thief who has stolen vital documents pertaining to the winner of the scholarship, but what will he do when the prime suspect is found dead? The story was inspired by the original story in the canon, *The Three Students.*

A Most Grave Ritual. In 1649, King Charles I escaped from the palace in which he was being held prisoner and made a desperate run for Southampton, hoping to reach safety on the Continent. He never made it and was returned to face trial and execution. Did he leave behind a vast fortune that he had taken from the Royal Treasury?

The Musgrave family now owns the old castle where the king may have left his fortune. The patriarch of the family dies in the courtyard and the locals believe that the headless ghost of the king did him in. The police accuse his son of murdering him so he could claim the fortune. Sherlock Holmes is hired to exonerate the lad.

The Stock Market Murders. A young man's friend has gone missing. Holmes and Watson go with him to Birmingham to help look for him. What they find is horrifying. Two more bodies of young men turn up in London. All of the victims are tied to Cambridge University. All are also tied to the financial sector of the City and to one of the greatest frauds ever visited upon the citizens of England. The story is based on the true story of James Whitaker Wright and is inspired by the original Sherlock Holmes story, *The Stock Broker's Clerk*. Any resemblance of the villain to a certain presidential candidate is entirely coincidental.

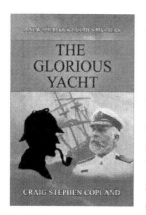

A Scandal in Trumplandia. Was Sherlock Holmes inadvertently responsible for the results of the election on November 8, 2016? This light-hearted parody (Note: NOT a New Sherlock Holmes mystery) reveals the secret meeting held between Sherlock Holmes and the GOP candidate for President of the United States. A devastating old film clip, made fifty years ago, if it is released, will completely destroy the campaign of The D—. Only Sherlock Holmes can save him from self-destruction. But will he want to? And, if so, will he be successful? The story is a parody of the much-loved original story, *A Scandal in Bohemia*, with the character of the King of Bohemia replaced by you-know-who. If you enjoy both political satire and Sherlock Holmes, you will get a chuckle out of this new story.

Reverend Ezekiel Black—'The Sherlock Holmes of the American West'—Mystery Stories.

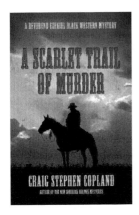

A Scarlet Trail of Murder. At ten o'clock on Sunday morning, the twenty-second of October, 1882, in an abandoned house in the West Bottom of Kansas City, a fellow named Jasper Harrison did not wake up. His inability to do was the result of his having had his throat cut sometime during the previous night. At the same time, in the same location, Eddie Kepler did wake up. Eddie staggered out into the blinding daylight and started hollering very loudly for the police. I know these things because by noon on that same day, I was kneeling down on the floor beside my new partner, the Reverend Mister Ezekiel Amos Black, and together we were examining the body of Mr. Jasper Harrison. Three weeks and nearly three thousand miles later, the Rev had not only brought the murderer to justice but had helped solve several other murders and some very nasty deeds that stretched back over fifteen years. This story of mine, written so as to be appropriate to all members of your family, about the brainiest and downright strangest preacher and part-time Deputy US Marshal, is going to tell you how that all came about. And I am not going to be at all surprised if, after reading it, you will agree with me that Reverend Ezekiel Black was certainly one very smart man but, my goodness, was he a strange bird.   Jim Watson, MD

This original western mystery was inspired by The great Sherlock Holmes classic, *A Study in Scarlet.*

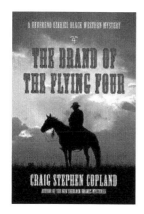

The Brand of the Flying Four. This case all began one quiet evening—very quiet; bordering on boring—while we were sitting by the hearth in our rooms in Kansas City. A few weeks later, a murder, perhaps the most gruesome I had ever witnessed in all my born days, took place in Denver, immediately above our heads. By the time it all ended, justice, of the frontier variety, not the courtroom, had been meted out. If you want to know how it all happened, you'll have to read this story. Jim Watson, M.D. Denver, 1883

The story is inspired by *The Sign of the Four"* by Arthur Conan Doyle, and like that story it combines murder most foul, and romance most enticing.

Collection Sets for ebooks– each with several more new Sherlock Holmes mysteries – are available as boxed sets at *40% off the price of buying them separately.*

Collection One

The Sign of the Third

The Hudson Valley Mystery

A Case of Identity Theft

The Bald-Headed Trust

Studying Scarlet

The Mystery of the Five Oranges

Collection Two

A Sandal from East Anglia

The Man Who Was Twisted But Hip

The Blue Belt Buckle

The Spectred Bat

Collection Three

The Engineer's Mom

The Notable Bachelorette

The Beryl Anarchists

The Coiffured Bitches

Collection Four

The Silver Horse, Braised

The Box of Cards

The Yellow Farce

The Three Rhodes Not Taken

As our way of thanking you for purchasing this book, you can now download six more new Sherlock Holmes mysteries for free.

Go now to

www.SherlockHolmesMystery.com, subscribe to Craig Stephen Copland's Irregular Newsletter, get six new mysteries FREE, and start enjoying more Sherlock now.

The Reigate Squires

The Original Sherlock Holmes Story

Arthur Conan Doyle

The Reigate Squires

The Original Sherlock Holmes Mystery

It was some time before the health of my friend Mr. Sherlock Holmes recovered from the strain caused by his immense exertions in the spring of '87. The whole question of the Netherland-Sumatra Company and of the colossal schemes of Baron Maupertuis are too recent in the minds of the public, and are too intimately concerned with politics and finance to be fitting subjects for this series of sketches. They led, however, in an indirect fashion to a singular and complex problem which gave my friend an opportunity of demonstrating the value of a fresh weapon among the many with which he waged his life-long battle against crime.

On referring to my notes I see that it was upon the 14th of April that I received a telegram from Lyons which informed me that Holmes was lying ill in the Hotel Dulong. Within twenty-four hours I was in his sick-room, and was relieved to find that there was nothing formidable in his symptoms. Even his iron constitution, however, had broken down under the strain of an investigation which had extended over two months, during which period he had never worked less than fifteen hours a day, and had more than once, as he assured me, kept to his task for five days at a stretch. Even the triumphant issue of his labors could not save him from reaction after so terrible an exertion, and at a time when Europe was ringing with his name and when his room was literally ankle-deep with congratulatory telegrams I found him a prey to the blackest depression. Even the knowledge that he had succeeded where the police of three countries had failed, and that he had outmanoeuvred at every point the most accomplished swindler in Europe, was insufficient to rouse him from his nervous prostration.

Three days later we were back in Baker Street together; but it was evident that my friend would be much the better for a change, and the thought of a week of spring time in the country was full of attractions to me also. My old friend, Colonel Hayter, who had come under my professional care in Afghanistan, had now taken a house near Reigate in Surrey, and had frequently asked me to come down to him upon a visit. On the last occasion he had remarked that if my friend would only come with me he would be glad to extend his hospitality to him also. A little diplomacy was needed, but when Holmes understood that the establishment was a bachelor one, and that he would be allowed the fullest freedom, he fell in with my plans and a week after our return from Lyons we were under the Colonel's roof. Hayter was a fine old soldier who had seen much of the world, and he soon found, as I had expected, that Holmes and he had much in common.

On the evening of our arrival we were sitting in the Colonel's gun-room after dinner, Holmes stretched upon the sofa, while Hayter and I looked over his little armory of Eastern weapons.

"By the way," said he suddenly, "I think I'll take one of these pistols upstairs with me in case we have an alarm."

"An alarm!" said I.

"Yes, we've had a scare in this part lately. Old Acton, who is one of our county magnates, had his house broken into last Monday. No great damage done, but the fellows are still at large."

"No clue?" asked Holmes, cocking his eye at the Colonel.

"None as yet. But the affair is a petty one, one of our little country crimes, which must seem too small for your attention, Mr. Holmes, after this great international affair."

Holmes waved away the compliment, though his smile showed that it had pleased him.

"Was there any feature of interest?"

"I fancy not. The thieves ransacked the library and got very little for their pains. The whole place was turned upside down, drawers burst open, and presses ransacked, with the result that an odd volume of Pope's "Homer," two plated candlesticks, an ivory letter-weight, a small oak barometer, and a ball of twine are all that have vanished."

"What an extraordinary assortment!" I exclaimed.

"Oh, the fellows evidently grabbed hold of everything they could get."

Holmes grunted from the sofa.

"The county police ought to make something of that," said he; "why, it is surely obvious that—"

But I held up a warning finger.

"You are here for a rest, my dear fellow. For Heaven's sake don't get started on a new problem when your nerves are all in shreds."

Holmes shrugged his shoulders with a glance of comic resignation towards the Colonel, and the talk drifted away into less dangerous channels.

It was destined, however, that all my professional caution should be wasted, for next morning the problem obtruded itself upon us in such a way that it was impossible to ignore it, and our country visit took a turn which neither of us could have anticipated. We were at breakfast when the Colonel's butler rushed in with all his propriety shaken out of him.

"Have you heard the news, sir?" he gasped. "At the Cunningham's sir!"

"Burglary!" cried the Colonel, with his coffee-cup in mid-air.

"Murder!"

The Colonel whistled. "By Jove!" said he. "Who's killed, then? The J.P. or his son?"

"Neither, sir. It was William the coachman. Shot through the heart, sir, and never spoke again."

"Who shot him, then?"

"The burglar, sir. He was off like a shot and got clean away. He'd just broke in at the pantry window when William came on him and met his end in saving his master's property."

"What time?"

"It was last night, sir, somewhere about twelve."

"Ah, then, we'll step over afterwards," said the Colonel, coolly settling down to his breakfast again. "It's a baddish business," he added when the butler had gone; "he's our leading man about here, is old Cunningham, and a very decent fellow too. He'll be cut up over this, for the man has been in his service for years and was a good servant. It's evidently the same villains who broke into Acton's."

"And stole that very singular collection," said Holmes, thoughtfully.

114

"Precisely."

"Hum! It may prove the simplest matter in the world, but all the same at first glance this is just a little curious, is it not? A gang of burglars acting in the country might be expected to vary the scene of their operations, and not to crack two cribs in the same district within a few days. When you spoke last night of taking precautions I remember that it passed through my mind that this was probably the last parish in England to which the thief or thieves would be likely to turn their attention—which shows that I have still much to learn."

"I fancy it's some local practitioner," said the Colonel. "In that case, of course, Acton's and Cunningham's are just the places he would go for, since they are far the largest about here."

"And richest?"

"Well, they ought to be, but they've had a lawsuit for some years which has sucked the blood out of both of them, I fancy. Old Acton has some claim on half Cunningham's estate, and the lawyers have been at it with both hands."

"If it's a local villain there should not be much difficulty in running him down," said Holmes with a yawn. "All right, Watson, I don't intend to meddle."

"Inspector Forrester, sir," said the butler, throwing open the door.

The official, a smart, keen-faced young fellow, stepped into the room. "Good-morning, Colonel," said he; "I hope I don't intrude, but we hear that Mr. Holmes of Baker Street is here."

The Colonel waved his hand towards my friend, and the Inspector bowed.

"We thought that perhaps you would care to step across, Mr. Holmes."

"The fates are against you, Watson," said he, laughing. "We were chatting about the matter when you came in, Inspector. Perhaps you can let us have a few details." As he leaned back in his chair in the familiar attitude I knew that the case was hopeless.

"We had no clue in the Acton affair. But here we have plenty to go on, and there's no doubt it is the same party in each case. The man was seen."

"Ah!"

"Yes, sir. But he was off like a deer after the shot that killed poor William Kirwan was fired. Mr. Cunningham saw him from the bedroom window, and Mr. Alec Cunningham saw him from the back passage. It was quarter to twelve when the alarm broke out. Mr. Cunningham had just got into bed, and Mr. Alec was smoking a pipe in his dressing-gown. They both heard William the coachman calling for help, and Mr. Alec ran down to see what was the matter. The back door was open, and as he came to the foot of the stairs he saw two men wrestling together outside. One of them fired a shot, the other dropped, and the murderer rushed across the garden and over the hedge. Mr. Cunningham, looking out of his bedroom, saw the fellow as he gained the road, but lost sight of him at once. Mr. Alec stopped to see if he could help the dying man, and so the villain got clean away. Beyond the fact that he was a middle-sized man and dressed in some dark stuff, we have no personal clue; but we are making energetic inquiries, and if he is a stranger we shall soon find him out."

"What was this William doing there? Did he say anything before he died?"

"Not a word. He lives at the lodge with his mother, and as he was a very faithful fellow we imagine that he walked up to the house with the intention of seeing that all was right there. Of course this Acton business has put every one on their guard. The robber must

116

have just burst open the door—the lock has been forced—when William came upon him."

"Did William say anything to his mother before going out?"

"She is very old and deaf, and we can get no information from her. The shock has made her half-witted, but I understand that she was never very bright. There is one very important circumstance, however. Look at this!"

He took a small piece of torn paper from a note-book and spread it out upon his knee.

"This was found between the finger and thumb of the dead man. It appears to be a fragment torn from a larger sheet. You will observe that the hour mentioned upon it is the very time at which the poor fellow met his fate. You see that his murderer might have torn the rest of the sheet from him or he might have taken this fragment from the murderer. It reads almost as though it were an appointment."

Holmes took up the scrap of paper, a fac-simile of which is here reproduced.

at quarter to twelve learn what may

"Presuming that it is an appointment," continued the Inspector, "it is of course a conceivable theory that this William Kirwan— though he had the reputation of being an honest man, may have been in league with the thief. He may have met him there, may even have helped him to break in the door, and then they may have fallen out between themselves."

"This writing is of extraordinary interest," said Holmes, who had been examining it with intense concentration. "These are much deeper waters than I had thought." He sank his head upon his hands, while the Inspector smiled at the effect which his case had had upon the famous London specialist.

"Your last remark," said Holmes, presently, "as to the possibility of there being an understanding between the burglar and the servant, and this being a note of appointment from one to the other, is an ingenious and not entirely impossible supposition. But this writing opens up—" He sank his head into his hands again and remained for some minutes in the deepest thought. When he raised his face again, I was surprised to see that his cheek was tinged with color, and his eyes as bright as before his illness. He sprang to his feet with all his old energy.

"I'll tell you what," said he, "I should like to have a quiet little glance into the details of this case. There is something in it which fascinates me extremely. If you will permit me, Colonel, I will leave my friend Watson and you, and I will step round with the Inspector to test the truth of one or two little fancies of mine. I will be with you again in half an hour."

An hour and half had elapsed before the Inspector returned alone.

"Mr. Holmes is walking up and down in the field outside," said he. "He wants us all four to go up to the house together."

"To Mr. Cunningham's?"

"Yes, sir."

"What for?"

The Inspector shrugged his shoulders. "I don't quite know, sir. Between ourselves, I think Mr. Holmes has not quite got over his illness yet. He's been behaving very queerly, and he is very much excited."

"I don't think you need alarm yourself," said I. "I have usually found that there was method in his madness."

"Some folks might say there was madness in his method," muttered the Inspector. "But he's all on fire to start, Colonel, so we had best go out if you are ready."

We found Holmes pacing up and down in the field, his chin sunk upon his breast, and his hands thrust into his trousers pockets.

"The matter grows in interest," said he. "Watson, your country-trip has been a distinct success. I have had a charming morning."

"You have been up to the scene of the crime, I understand," said the Colonel.

"Yes; the Inspector and I have made quite a little reconnaissance together."

"Any success?"

"Well, we have seen some very interesting things. I'll tell you what we did as we walk. First of all, we saw the body of this unfortunate man. He certainly died from a revolver wound as reported."

"Had you doubted it, then?"

"Oh, it is as well to test everything. Our inspection was not wasted. We then had an interview with Mr. Cunningham and his son, who were able to point out the exact spot where the murderer had broken through the garden-hedge in his flight. That was of great interest."

"Naturally."

"Then we had a look at this poor fellow's mother. We could get no information from her, however, as she is very old and feeble."

"And what is the result of your investigations?"

"The conviction that the crime is a very peculiar one. Perhaps our visit now may do something to make it less obscure. I think that we are both agreed, Inspector that the fragment of paper in the dead man's hand, bearing, as it does, the very hour of his death written upon it, is of extreme importance."

"It should give a clue, Mr. Holmes."

"It does give a clue. Whoever wrote that note was the man who brought William Kirwan out of his bed at that hour. But where is the rest of that sheet of paper?"

"I examined the ground carefully in the hope of finding it," said the Inspector.

"It was torn out of the dead man's hand. Why was some one so anxious to get possession of it? Because it incriminated him. And what would he do with it? Thrust it into his pocket, most likely, never noticing that a corner of it had been left in the grip of the corpse. If we could get the rest of that sheet it is obvious that we should have gone a long way towards solving the mystery."

"Yes, but how can we get at the criminal's pocket before we catch the criminal?"

"Well, well, it was worth thinking over. Then there is another obvious point. The note was sent to William. The man who wrote it could not have taken it; otherwise, of course, he might have delivered his own message by word of mouth. Who brought the note, then? Or did it come through the post?"

"I have made inquiries," said the Inspector. "William received a letter by the afternoon post yesterday. The envelope was destroyed by him."

"Excellent!" cried Holmes, clapping the Inspector on the back. "You've seen the postman. It is a pleasure to work with you. Well, here is the lodge, and if you will come up, Colonel, I will show you the scene of the crime."

We passed the pretty cottage where the murdered man had lived, and walked up an oak-lined avenue to the fine old Queen Anne house, which bears the date of Malplaquet upon the lintel of the door. Holmes and the Inspector led us round it until we came to the side gate, which is separated by a stretch of garden from the hedge which lines the road. A constable was standing at the kitchen door.

"Throw the door open, officer," said Holmes. "Now, it was on those stairs that young Mr. Cunningham stood and saw the two men struggling just where we are. Old Mr. Cunningham was at that window—the second on the left—and he saw the fellow get away just to the left of that bush. Then Mr. Alec ran out and knelt beside the wounded man. The ground is very hard, you see, and there are no marks to guide us." As he spoke two men came down the garden path, from round the angle of the house. The one was an elderly man, with a strong, deep-lined, heavy-eyed face; the other a dashing young fellow, whose bright, smiling expression and showy dress were in strange contract with the business which had brought us there.

"Still at it, then?" said he to Holmes. "I thought you Londoners were never at fault. You don't seem to be so very quick, after all."

"Ah, you must give us a little time," said Holmes good-humoredly.

"You'll want it," said young Alec Cunningham. "Why, I don't see that we have any clue at all."

"There's only one," answered the Inspector. "We thought that if we could only find—Good heavens, Mr. Holmes! What is the matter?"

man accidentally tipping table over

My poor friend's face had suddenly assumed the most dreadful expression. His eyes rolled upwards, his features writhed in agony, and with a suppressed groan he dropped on his face upon the ground. Horrified at the suddenness and severity of the attack, we carried him into the kitchen, where he lay back in a large chair, and breathed heavily for some minutes. Finally, with a shamefaced apology for his weakness, he rose once more.

"Watson would tell you that I have only just recovered from a severe illness," he explained. "I am liable to these sudden nervous attacks."

"Shall I send you home in my trap?" asked old Cunningham.

"Well, since I am here, there is one point on which I should like to feel sure. We can very easily verify it."

"What was it?"

"Well, it seems to me that it is just possible that the arrival of this poor fellow William was not before, but after, the entrance of the burglary into the house. You appear to take it for granted that, although the door was forced, the robber never got in."

"I fancy that is quite obvious," said Mr. Cunningham, gravely. "Why, my son Alec had not yet gone to bed, and he would certainly have heard any one moving about."

"Where was he sitting?"

"I was smoking in my dressing-room."

"Which window is that?"

"The last on the left next my father's."

"Both of your lamps were lit, of course?"

"Undoubtedly."

"There are some very singular points here," said Holmes, smiling. "Is it not extraordinary that a burglary—and a burglar who had had some previous experience—should deliberately break into a house at a time when he could see from the lights that two of the family were still afoot?"

"He must have been a cool hand."

"Well, of course, if the case were not an odd one we should not have been driven to ask you for an explanation," said young Mr. Alec. "But as to your ideas that the man had robbed the house before William tackled him, I think it a most absurd notion. Wouldn't we have found the place disarranged, and missed the things which he had taken?"

"It depends on what the things were," said Holmes. "You must remember that we are dealing with a burglar who is a very peculiar fellow, and who appears to work on lines of his own. Look, for example, at the queer lot of things which he took from Acton's—what was it?—a ball of string, a letter-weight, and I don't know what other odds and ends."

"Well, we are quite in your hands, Mr. Holmes," said old Cunningham. "Anything which you or the Inspector may suggest will most certainly be done."

"In the first place," said Holmes, "I should like you to offer a reward—coming from yourself, for the officials may take a little time before they would agree upon the sum, and these things cannot be done too promptly. I have jotted down the form here, if you would not mind signing it. Fifty pounds was quite enough, I thought."

"I would willingly give five hundred," said the J.P., taking the slip of paper and the pencil which Holmes handed to him. "This is not quite correct, however," he added, glancing over the document.

"I wrote it rather hurriedly."

"You see you begin, 'Whereas, at about a quarter to one on Tuesday morning an attempt was made,' and so on. It was at a quarter to twelve, as a matter of fact."

I was pained at the mistake, for I knew how keenly Holmes would feel any slip of the kind. It was his specialty to be accurate as to fact, but his recent illness had shaken him, and this one little incident was enough to show me that he was still far from being himself. He was obviously embarrassed for an instant, while the Inspector raised his eyebrows, and Alec Cunningham burst into a laugh. The old gentleman corrected the mistake, however, and handed the paper back to Holmes.

"Get it printed as soon as possible," he said; "I think your idea is an excellent one."

Holmes put the slip of paper carefully away into his pocket-book.

"And now," said he, "it really would be a good thing that we should all go over the house together and make certain that this rather erratic burglar did not, after all, carry anything away with him."

Before entering, Holmes made an examination of the door which had been forced. It was evident that a chisel or strong knife had been thrust in, and the lock forced back with it. We could see the marks in the wood where it had been pushed in.

"You don't use bars, then?" he asked.

"We have never found it necessary."

"You don't keep a dog?"

"Yes, but he is chained on the other side of the house."

"When do the servants go to bed?"

"About ten."

"I understand that William was usually in bed also at that hour."

"Yes."

"It is singular that on this particular night he should have been up. Now, I should be very glad if you would have the kindness to show us over the house, Mr. Cunningham."

A stone-flagged passage, with the kitchens branching away from it, led by a wooden staircase directly to the first floor of the house. It came out upon the landing opposite to a second more ornamental stair which came up from the front hall. Out of this landing opened the drawing-room and several bedrooms, including those of Mr. Cunningham and his son. Holmes walked slowly, taking keen note of the architecture of the house. I could tell from his expression that he was on a hot scent, and yet I could not in the least imagine in what direction his inferences were leading him.

"My good sir," said Mr. Cunningham with some impatience, "this is surely very unnecessary. That is my room at the end of the stairs, and my son's is the one beyond it. I leave it to your judgment whether it was possible for the thief to have come up here without disturbing us."

"You must try round and get on a fresh scent, I fancy," said the son with a rather malicious smile.

"Still, I must ask you to humor me a little further. I should like, for example, to see how far the windows of the bedrooms command the front. This, I understand is your son's room"—he pushed open the door—"and that, I presume, is the dressing-room in which he sat smoking when the alarm was given. Where does the window of that look out to?" He stepped across the bedroom, pushed open the door, and glanced round the other chamber.

"I hope that you are satisfied now?" said Mr. Cunningham, tartly.

"Thank you, I think I have seen all that I wished."

"Then if it is really necessary we can go into my room."

"If it is not too much trouble."

The J. P. shrugged his shoulders, and led the way into his own chamber, which was a plainly furnished and commonplace room. As we moved across it in the direction of the window, Holmes fell back until he and I were the last of the group. Near the foot of the bed stood a dish of oranges and a carafe of water. As we passed it Holmes, to my unutterable astonishment, leaned over in front of me and deliberately knocked the whole thing over. The glass smashed into a thousand pieces and the fruit rolled about into every corner of the room.

"You've done it now, Watson," said he, coolly. "A pretty mess you've made of the carpet."

I stooped in some confusion and began to pick up the fruit, understanding for some reason my companion desired me to take the blame upon myself. The others did the same, and set the table on its legs again.

"Hullo!" cried the Inspector, "where's he got to?"

Holmes had disappeared.

"Wait here an instant," said young Alec Cunningham. "The fellow is off his head, in my opinion. Come with me, father, and see where he has got to!"

They rushed out of the room, leaving the Inspector, the Colonel, and me staring at each other.

"'Pon my word, I am inclined to agree with Master Alec," said the official. "It may be the effect of this illness, but it seems to me that—"

His words were cut short by a sudden scream of "Help! Help! Murder!" With a thrill I recognized the voice of that of my friend. I rushed madly from the room on to the landing. The cries, which had sunk down into a hoarse, inarticulate shouting, came from the room which we had first visited. I dashed in, and on into the dressing-room beyond. The two Cunninghams were bending over the prostrate figure of Sherlock Holmes, the younger clutching his throat with both hands, while the elder seemed to be twisting one of his wrists. In an instant the three of us had torn them away from him, and Holmes staggered to his feet, very pale and evidently greatly exhausted.

"Arrest these men, Inspector," he gasped.

"On what charge?"

"That of murdering their coachman, William Kirwan."

The Inspector stared about him in bewilderment. "Oh, come now, Mr. Holmes," said he at last, "I'm sure you don't really mean to—"

"Tut, man, look at their faces!" cried Holmes, curtly.

Never certainly have I seen a plainer confession of guilt upon human countenances. The older man seemed numbed and dazed with a heavy, sullen expression upon his strongly-marked face. The son, on the other hand, had dropped all that jaunty, dashing style which had characterized him, and the ferocity of a dangerous wild beast gleamed in his dark eyes and distorted his handsome features. The Inspector said nothing, but, stepping to the door, he blew his whistle. Two of his constables came at the call.

"I have no alternative, Mr. Cunningham," said he. "I trust that this may all prove to be an absurd mistake, but you can see that—Ah, would you? Drop it!" He struck out with his hand, and a revolver which the younger man was in the act of cocking clattered down upon the floor.

"Keep that," said Holmes, quietly putting his foot upon it; "you will find it useful at the trial. But this is what we really wanted." He held up a little crumpled piece of paper.

"The remainder of the sheet!" cried the Inspector.

"Precisely."

"And where was it?"

"Where I was sure it must be. I'll make the whole matter clear to you presently. I think, Colonel, that you and Watson might return now, and I will be with you again in an hour at the furthest. The Inspector and I must have a word with the prisoners, but you will certainly see me back at luncheon time."

Sherlock Holmes was as good as his word, for about one o'clock he rejoined us in the Colonel's smoking-room. He was accompanied by a little elderly gentleman, who was introduced to me as the Mr. Acton whose house had been the scene of the original burglary.

"I wished Mr. Acton to be present while I demonstrated this small matter to you," said Holmes, "for it is natural that he should take a keen interest in the details. I am afraid, my dear Colonel, that you must regret the hour that you took in such a stormy petrel as I am."

"On the contrary," answered the Colonel, warmly, "I consider it the greatest privilege to have been permitted to study your methods of working. I confess that they quite surpass my expectations, and that I am utterly unable to account for your result. I have not yet seen the vestige of a clue."

"I am afraid that my explanation may disillusion you but it has always been my habit to hide none of my methods, either from my friend Watson or from any one who might take an intelligent interest in them. But, first, as I am rather shaken by the knocking about which I had in the dressing-room, I think that I shall help myself to a dash of your brandy, Colonel. My strength had been rather tried of late."

"I trust that you had no more of those nervous attacks."

Sherlock Holmes laughed heartily. "We will come to that in its turn," said he. "I will lay an account of the case before you in its due order, showing you the various points which guided me in my decision. Pray interrupt me if there is any inference which is not perfectly clear to you.

"It is of the highest importance in the art of detection to be able to recognize, out of a number of facts, which are incidental and which vital. Otherwise your energy and attention must be dissipated instead of being concentrated. Now, in this case there was not the slightest doubt in my mind from the first that the key of the whole matter must be looked for in the scrap of paper in the dead man's hand.

"Before going into this, I would draw your attention to the fact that, if Alec Cunningham's narrative was correct, and if the assailant, after shooting William Kirwan, had instantly fled, then it obviously could not be he who tore the paper from the dead man's hand. But if it was not he, it must have been Alec Cunningham himself, for by the time that the old man had descended several servants were upon the scene. The point is a simple one, but the Inspector had overlooked it because he had started with the supposition that these county magnates had had nothing to do with the matter. Now, I make a point of never having any prejudices, and of following docilely wherever fact may lead me, and so, in the very first stage of the investigation, I found myself looking a little askance at the part which had been played by Mr. Alec Cunningham.

"And now I made a very careful examination of the corner of paper which the Inspector had submitted to us. It was at once clear to me that it formed part of a very remarkable document. Here it is. Do you not now observe something very suggestive about it?"

"It has a very irregular look," said the Colonel.

"My dear sir," cried Holmes, "there cannot be the least doubt in the world that it has been written by two persons doing alternate words. When I draw your attention to the strong t's of 'at' and 'to', and ask you to compare them with the weak ones of 'quarter' and 'twelve,' you will instantly recognize the fact. A very brief analysis of these four words would enable you to say with the utmost confidence that the 'learn' and the 'maybe' are written in the stronger hand, and the 'what' in the weaker."

"By Jove, it's as clear as day!" cried the Colonel. "Why on earth should two men write a letter in such a fashion?"

"Obviously the business was a bad one, and one of the men who distrusted the other was determined that, whatever was done, each should have an equal hand in it. Now, of the two men, it is clear that the one who wrote the 'at' and 'to' was the ringleader."

"How do you get at that?"

"We might deduce it from the mere character of the one hand as compared with the other. But we have more assured reasons than that for supposing it. If you examine this scrap with attention you will come to the conclusion that the man with the stronger hand wrote all his words first, leaving blanks for the other to fill up. These blanks were not always sufficient, and you can see that the second man had a squeeze to fit his 'quarter' in between the 'at' and the 'to,' showing that the latter were already written. The man who wrote all his words first is undoubtedly the man who planned the affair."

"Excellent!" cried Mr. Acton.

"But very superficial," said Holmes. "We come now, however, to a point which is of importance. You may not be aware that the deduction of a man's age from his writing is one which has brought to considerable accuracy by experts. In normal cases one can place a man in his true decade with tolerable confidence. I say normal cases, because ill-health and physical weakness reproduce the signs of old age, even when the invalid is a youth. In this case, looking at the bold, strong hand of the one, and the rather broken-backed appearance of the other, which still retains its legibility although the t's have begun to lose their crossing, we can say that the one was a young man and the other was advanced in years without being positively decrepit."

"Excellent!" cried Mr. Acton again.

"There is a further point, however, which is subtler and of greater interest. There is something in common between these hands. They belong to men who are blood-relatives. It may be most obvious to you in the Greek e's, but to me there are many small points which indicate the same thing. I have no doubt at all that a family mannerism can be traced in these two specimens of writing. I am only, of course, giving you the leading results now of my examination of the paper. There were twenty-three other deductions which would be of more interest to experts than to you. They all tend to deepen the impression upon my mind that the Cunninghams, father and son, had written this letter.

"Having got so far, my next step was, of course, to examine into the details of the crime, and to see how far they would help us. I went up to the house with the Inspector, and saw all that was to be seen. The wound upon the dead man was, as I was able to determine with absolute confidence, fired from a revolver at the distance of something over four yards. There was no powder-blackening on the clothes. Evidently, therefore, Alec Cunningham had lied when he said that the two men were struggling when the shot was fired. Again, both father and son agreed as to the place where the man escaped into the road. At that point, however, as it happens, there is a broadish ditch, moist at the bottom. As there were no indications of bootmarks about this ditch, I was absolutely sure not only that the Cunninghams had again lied, but that there had never been any man upon the scene at all.

"And now I have to consider the motive of this singular crime. To get at this, I endeavored first of all to solve the reason of the original burglary at Mr. Acton's. I understood, from something which the Colonel told us, that a lawsuit had been going on between you, Mr. Acton, and the Cunninghams. Of course, it instantly occurred to me that they had broken into your library with the intention of getting at some document which might be of importance in the case."

"Precisely so," said Mr. Acton. "There can be no possible doubt as to their intentions. I have the clearest claim upon half of their present estate, and if they could have found a single paper—which, fortunately, was in the strong-box of my solicitors—they would undoubtedly have crippled our case."

"There you are," said Holmes, smiling. "It was a dangerous, reckless attempt, in which I seem to trace the influence of young Alec. Having found nothing they tried to divert suspicion by making it appear to be an ordinary burglary, to which end they carried off whatever they could lay their hands upon. That is all clear enough, but there was much that was still obscure. What I wanted above all was to get the missing part of that note. I was certain that Alec had torn it out of the dead man's hand, and almost certain that he must have thrust it into the pocket of his dressing-gown. Where else could he have put it? The only question was whether it was still there. It was worth an effort to find out, and for that object we all went up to the house.

"The Cunninghams joined us, as you doubtless remember, outside the kitchen door. It was, of course, of the very first importance that they should not be reminded of the existence of this paper, otherwise they would naturally destroy it without delay. The Inspector was about to tell them the importance which we attached to it when, by the luckiest chance in the world, I tumbled down in a sort of fit and so changed the conversation.

"Good heavens!" cried the Colonel, laughing, "do you mean to say all our sympathy was wasted and your fit an imposture?"

"Speaking professionally, it was admirably done," cried I, looking in amazement at this man who was forever confounding me with some new phase of his astuteness.

"It is an art which is often useful," said he. "When I recovered I managed, by a device which had perhaps some little merit of ingenuity, to get old Cunningham to write the word 'twelve,' so that I might compare it with the 'twelve' upon the paper."

"Oh, what an ass I have been!" I exclaimed.

"I could see that you were commiserating me over my weakness," said Holmes, laughing. "I was sorry to cause you the sympathetic pain which I know that you felt. We then went upstairs together, and having entered the room and seen the dressing-gown hanging up behind the door, I contrived, by upsetting a table, to engage their attention for the moment, and slipped back to examine the pockets. I had hardly got the paper, however—which was, as I had expected, in one of them—when the two Cunninghams were on me, and would, I verily believe, have murdered me then and there but for your prompt and friendly aid. As it is, I feel that young man's grip on my throat now, and the father has twisted my wrist round in the effort to get the paper out of my hand. They saw that I must know all about it, you see, and the sudden change from absolute security to complete despair made them perfectly desperate.

"I had a little talk with old Cunningham afterwards as to the motive of the crime. He was tractable enough, though his son was a perfect demon, ready to blow out his own or anybody else's brains if he could have got to his revolver. When Cunningham saw that the case against him was so strong he lost all heart and made a clean breast of everything. It seems that William had secretly followed his two masters on the night when they made their raid upon Mr. Acton's, and having thus got them into his power, proceeded, under threats of exposure, to levy blackmail upon them. Mr. Alec, however, was a dangerous man to play games of that sort with. It was a stroke of positive genius on his part to see in the burglary scare which was convulsing the country side an opportunity of plausibly getting rid of the man whom he feared. William was decoyed up and shot, and had they only got the whole of the note and paid a little more attention to detail in the accessories, it is very possible that suspicion might never have been aroused."

"And the note?" I asked.

Sherlock Holmes placed the subjoined paper before us. If you will only come around at quarter to twelve to the east gate you will learn what will very much surprise you and may be of greatest service to you and also to Annie Morrison. But say nothing to anyong upon the matter

"It is very much the sort of thing that I expected," said he. "Of course, we do not yet know what the relations may have been between Alec Cunningham, William Kirwan, and Annie Morrison. The results shows that the trap was skillfully baited. I am sure that you cannot fail to be delighted with the traces of heredity shown in the p's and in the tails of the g's. The absence of the i-dots in the old man's writing is also most characteristic. Watson, I think our quiet rest in the country has been a distinct success, and I shall certainly return much invigorated to Baker Street to-morrow."

Made in the USA
San Bernardino, CA
28 April 2017